YuvaKatha

YuvaKatha ... an effort which is both aesthetically satisfying and politically correct.
— *The Hindu*

... for all those who enjoy a good book, keeping an eye out for this one would be worth the trouble.
— *The Hindustan Times*

The *YuvaKatha* series is an interesting blend ... pleasurable reading.
— *The Asian Age*

An unusual book, by several accounts.
— *The Hindustan Times*

Hello,
I'm Jaldi the Turtle.
I have been on Earth for millions of years.
I am a survivor!
So these Katha books on sustainable living
are named after me!
Write to me – won't you?

KATHA
has planted two trees
to replace the one tree that was used
to make the paper
on which this book is printed.

**Other Books
In the YuvaKatha Series**

Book One
Lukose's Church and Other Stories

Book Two
Night of the Third Crescent and Other Stories

Book Three
Bhiku's Diary and Other Stories

Book Four
The Verdict and Other Stories

Book Five
The Dragonfly and Other Stories

The
BELL
And Other Stories

Unforgettable
short fiction from some of
India's master storytellers

EDITED
BY
GEETA
DHARMARAJAN
AND
KEERTI
RAMACHANDRA

KATHA

Published by

KATHA

A-3 Sarvodaya Enclave
Sri Aurobindo Marg, New Delhi 110017
Phone: 652 4511, 652 4350, 686 8193, 652 1752
Fax: 651 4373
E-mail: katha@vsnl.com
Internet address: http://www.katha.org

Published by Katha in April, 2000
Second printing, May, 2001

Copyright © Katha, April, 2000
Copyright © for each individual story in its original language is held by the author. Copyright © for the English translations rests with KATHA.

KATHA is a registered nonprofit society devoted to enhancing the pleasures of reading. KATHA VILASAM is its story research and resource centre.

In-house Editors: Chandana Dutta, Shoma Choudhury, V Sri Ranjani
Book and Cover Design: Arvinder Chawla

Typeset in 10.5 on 14.5pt New Century Schl BT by Sandeep Kumar at Katha and Printed at Usha Offset, New Delhi

All rights reserved. No part of this book may be reproduced or utilized in any form or by any means, electronic or mechanical, including photocopying, recording or by any information storage or retrieval system, without the prior written permission of the publisher.

ISBN 81-85586-72-1 (Series)   ISBN 81-85586-71-3

Contents

The Bell by Gita Krishnankutty   7

Partition by Swayam Prakash   15
translated from Hindi by Madhavi Mahadevan & Kaveri Rastogi

The Blue Light by Vaikom Muhammed Basheer   27
translated from Malayalam by C P A Vasudevan

The Purple Haze by Vasudha Mane   43
translated from Marathi by the Author

Jalebis by Ahmed Nadeem Qasmi   53
translated from Urdu by Sufiya Pathan

Arjun by Mahasweta Devi   63
translated from Bangla by Mridula Nath Chakraborty

The Fishmonger by Bolwar Mahamad Kunhi   75
translated from Kannada by H Y Sharada Prasad

The Will by Ahmad Yusuf   91
translated from Urdu by Nadeem Ahmed

The Door by Himanshi Shelat   107
translated from Gujarati by Darshana Dave

Big Apple, Black Apple by Mridula Garg   115
translated from Hindi by Shalini Sharma

The
BELL
GITA KRISHNANKUTTY

An unusual sense of excitement pervaded her visit to the temple that evening. There had been an argument between her and the grown-ups at lunch time when she had announced her decision to ring the bell in front of the sanctuary at the hour of deeparadhana.

"If Thangam can ring it, so can I," she had argued hotly.

They had protested in shocked voices, "Thangam is the daughter of the temple priest. She is permitted to touch the bell."

Thangam came over to play hide-and-seek every afternoon, she had retorted and behaved no differently from any of them.

"Besides," she added, provoking them deliberately, "We are all equal in the eyes of God." She was not quite sure whether they had heard this bit, for they had already turned away in disgust. But after lunch she caught them whispering about "That horrid English school she goes to," which meant that they had heard ...

She was sure they had not taken her seriously. That was the trouble with grown-ups: they always presumed that if they told her that she would understand everything when she was older, she would accept their wisdom and authority unquestioningly and not dream of going against them. Well, this time, she would show them ...

And so, with good grace, she submitted to the suggestion that she accompany her grandmother to the tank for her evening bath, though she really preferred the makeshift bathroom at the back of the house. It had originally been a lumber-room. The old cardboard box that had once held the radio but was now crammed to bursting with old newspapers, magazines and broken toys, had simply been pushed to one side to accommodate a rickety wooden stool. On top of the stool was a chembu to hold the steaming grey water that smelt of smoke. She hated the slippery stone steps of the tank. The dark green slime at their edges menaced her foothold. The water had a sullen, dangerous look and always felt bitterly cold.

But she endured it all that day without complaint, chattering brightly. She did not fuss when the tiny fishes swarmed around her ankles, nipping at them viciously, threatening her precarious balance.

Back at the house, she had to undergo the intensely uncomfortable ritual of hair-dressing. They smoothed her hair with what seemed like a whole jar of oil, separated each shining strand till it hung limp, lifeless and straight down her back. Then it was pulled back, tied in a tight, skin-stretching knot on the top of her head and secured with a long strand of plantain stem fibre. She was thankful none of her school friends could see her like this. Droplets of oil oozing down her temples sent tiny shivers of disgust through her. The back of her neck felt slimy. She wished she could wriggle out of her skin. But she bit back her annoyance, contenting herself with a savage swipe at her oily forehead with the edge of her skirt when they were not looking.

She was ready before the evening flurry of lamp-

The Bell

lighting started. The old, toothless major-domo of the household, Kelu Nair, was instructed to accompany her. Why couldn't they understand how ridiculous she felt, escorted by him? She had reminded her mother so many times that she walked alone to school every day when they were back in the town, that she even went by herself to the bakery at the end of the road to buy sweets and cakes. Her mother simply pretended not to hear. She alternately envied and detested the grown-ups for their loathsome habit of not hearing whatever they found inconvenient to answer.

On some days, when she was able to strike a strategic blend of authority and appeal, she could induce Kelu Nair to walk a few steps behind her. Then she pretended that he did not belong to her at all. But it was something she rarely achieved. That evening Kelu Nair stuck obstinately to her side, imparting bits and pieces of information and advice which she tried to ignore. She quickened her steps as they reached the road, almost breaking into a run. Kelu Nair shouted at her to stop and wait for him. She did not care to explain to anyone that she tried to cover this stretch of road as quickly as possible because the rough gravel hurt her bare feet.

Once she reached the temple entrance she slowed down, grateful for the feel of smooth, sun-warmed stone.

The usual knot of women had gathered around the three-tiered stone lamp at the outer gate, talking earnestly in hushed voices, their faces grave and sad. Kelu Nair edged as close to them as he dared. She knew he drank in every whisper that he could distinguish, so that he could impart it all, embellished with many scandalous details of his own invention, to her mother and grandmother over dinner later at night.

As they started the ritual circling of the outer walls of the temple, she noticed that the football game had already begun in the courtyard beside the sanctuary of Krishna. She enjoyed watching the players, more so because her obvious delight in the vigour of their game, and in the raucously-voiced comments that she was not meant to overhear, irritated Kelu Nair profoundly.

When they arrived at the sanctuary of Krishna, she saw that the small, low door, which the priest must certainly fold himself in half to pass through, was, as usual, obstinately shut. Kelu Nair had told her time and again that the idol inside was infinitely more beautiful than the one at Guruvayoor. She had tried hard to find out when he had seen it, for the sanctum had never been open as far as she could remember. Kelu Nair was extremely evasive on this question, but he insisted that he had seen it, and that it was ah, so lovely, especially when it was decorated with sandal paste and flowers. Sometimes, when he was annoyed with her, he would hint darkly that perhaps she was not worthy of seeing it.

She circled the shrine hurriedly that day, her mind full of her secret mission. She almost ran along the long, unbroken northern wall, inviting an incomprehensible torrent of protests from Kelu Nair, who could not keep up with her.

The eastern facade of the temple always enchanted her. Whenever she thought about it afterwards, as she often did, her memories were full of sound and colour. The river ran through there, the jade green of its water melting imperceptibly first into the rice field beyond and then into the luminous evening sky. In the enclosed area where the women bathed, shrill voices rose above the wet slapping of cloth against stone. The gory details of the calving of someone's black cow dovetailed into a steady drone of devout chanting. A stream of women, young and old, in freshly-washed clothes, wringing the water out of their damp hair, flowed from the low, tiled halls. She loved the way the shapes of bodies outlined themselves sharply through the wet, white curtains of fabric hanging about their shoulders.

On the other, unsheltered side of the river, young men dived and swam, thumping each other on the back, their voices loud, deliberately arrogant. Old men sunned themselves sleepily on the rough, rock-hewn steps leading down to the water. Pigeons whirled and cooed on the ledges, the walls. The big pillared hall on the river side eternally smelt of their droppings. In the evening sunlight their incredible loveliness as they wheeled over the conical gopuram, clutched at her heart making her almost forget her mission. But only for an instant. Quickly she ran through the hall, skipping over pigeon droppings, to the tiny temple of Bhagavati, perched high on a rock above the river. Standing on the narrow ledge to make her obeisance always exhilarated her. She felt splendidly isolated there, poised breathtakingly between earth and sky. The bathers in the river were just floating voices, the pigeons flashing grey-blue-green in a sky she could touch with her fingertips ...

But the rock beneath her feet was turning cool. The hour of deeparadhana was near. She hurried back through the shadow-filled hall. Beyond the tall golden flagpole tiny pinpoints of light pierced the warm darkness of the inner sanctuary. The first tentative beats of the edakka sounded unbelievably pure in a dusk filled with pigeons' wings. She touched the flagpole three times for luck, ran swiftly past the last, the southern wall, barely bowing her head in hasty obeisance to the yakshis beneath the banyan tree whom she never failed to propitiate. Kelu Nair, muttering angrily, was close upon her heels. Rounding the wall, she acknowledged with an involuntary intake of breath the sparkling rectangle of brightness that outlined the door of the corner sanctuary of Ayyappa ...

Inside the temple her feet lovingly caressed the cool stone of the inner courtyard revelling in its smooth worn feel. She bowed a perfunctory greeting to the little doll-like Parvati, crossed her arms and touched her ears before the dark, almost invisible Ganesha, and hurried towards the crowded main sanctuary. A familiar scent of hot oil and flowers, of vibhuti and wet clothes, welcomed her. The women of the Namboodiri household stood in front, in a tight invincible circle that no one must touch, clutching their thatch umbrellas that obscured everyone's vision, their eyes closed, their lips moving in an ecstasy of prayer. She edged her way towards them, ignoring Kelu Nair's shocked protestations, almost bumping into one of the ridiculous umbrellas. She saw Thangam standing near the steps, looking remote and rapt with devotion.

The rhythm of the edakka was mounting crazily. Suddenly the door was flung open. She blinked at the sudden vision of gold. Before she could regret her decision or go back upon it, she elbowed through the untouchable circle of Namboodiri women, almost floundering on the slippery steps. She could hear Kelu

The Bell

Nair's frantic, hoarsely whispered threats. But she saw only the big bell above. It filled her with a heady excitement. She reached up, pushed the bell with one resounding clang and was down the steps before anyone realized what was happening.

She was dimly aware of dark looks and subdued murmurs pursuing her as she allowed Kelu Nair to drag her away.

As they returned home in the gathering shadows, his imprecations grew louder and more vehement. Warnings of her great-grandmother's terrible wrath became inextricably mixed up with grim forebodings for her own spiritual salvation. She paid no heed to any of it. She felt wondrously light-hearted, excitingly happy. As she climbed over the stone stile to enter the house, she turned for a last look at the temple. It gleamed back at her conspiratorially, blessing her happiness.

She was in dire disgrace. Their tight-lipped silence was infinitely more eloquent than speech, as was the conspicuous absence of the tiny pappadams, her favourites, at dinner. The pappadams were specially ordered for her every holiday and served regularly at every meal.

She did not really care. For the silence seemed peopled with a thousand voices singing within her. And she was quite, quite sure that the golden god within the temple, in whose eyes all are equal, had accepted her gesture with love.

PARTITION
SWAYAM PRAKASH

translated from Hindi by Madhavi Mahadevan and Kaveri Rastogi

Do you know Qurban bhai? He is the most remarkable person in our kasba. The heart of this kasba is Azad Chowk. And that is where Qurban bhai has a small grocery shop.

It is not a big shop. But it is usually quite busy. You will find Qurban bhai, dressed as always, in a white kurta pyjama, surrounded by customers demanding a few paise worth of this or that. And if there is no crowd, you will probably see him sitting cross-legged on the floor, engrossed in writing. As he writes, he frequently runs his fingers through his hair. Every now and then he pushes back the thick-framed spectacles that keep sliding down the bridge of his nose.

If you wish to be his customer you will be more than welcome. Value for money and pure unadulterated stuff is what you can expect. If Qurban bhai is not sure about the quality of any item in his shop, rest assured he will not sell it. It may as well lie there and rot. He has even been heard saying things like, Chilli powder? No, don't buy this stuff. It has artificial colour mixed in it. Oil? Take this, but don't use it for cooking. It lacks flavour. It has been mixed with rapeseed oil. If you are going to buy it, use it for the lamp.

It is hardly surprising, then, that anyone who makes a purchase at his shop even once, becomes a regular customer. There are several big stores in the neighbourhood, owned by Sindhis and Marwaris. But Qurban bhai has a unique reputation. He stands for honesty, reliability and the convenience of Buy now, Pay later.

If you ever buy anything at Qurban bhai's shop don't throw the paper bag away, carelessly, without even a glance at it. In all probability you will find a pithy and powerful Urdu couplet written on it. Many people have advised Qurban bhai to keep a notebook at hand so that whenever inspiration seizes him, he can promptly put down his thoughts. Qurban bhai always listens patiently to this suggestion, agrees politely with it, even laments lost opportunities. But he does exactly as before.

My introduction to this wonderful man came about in an interesting manner. One day while returning from office I stopped at the shop to buy a few things. When I reached home I noticed these lines on the bag:

> *The only wealth I have is my loyalty.*
> *But for it, everything would be within reach*
> *The raging fury of Anger can be extinguished ...*
> *Within me is a reservoir of tolerance ...*

And the man who is capable of such thoughts runs his little grocery shop. Even today. There is a story behind this too.

Qurban bhai was born into a wealthy family. His father ran a flourishing business in dyes and colours in Ajmer. They owned two havelis and a big shop in Naya

Partition

Bazaar. Besides a buggy, they possessed a Baby Austin used only for leisurely drives. Maulana Azad was a close friend of the family. Eminent political leaders, poets and other intellectuals of that time often visited their haveli. In those days Qurban bhai was a student at Aligarh Muslim University. Life was extremely pleasant – romance, poetry, dreams!

And then came the Partition.

In its wake there were communal riots. The shop in Naya Bazaar was set on fire. Qurban bhai's relatives left for Pakistan. Qurban bhai had two brothers. Both were murdered. Unable to bear the grief, their father too, passed away. The house was looted by the servants who then ran away. Qurban bhai gathered the few belongings that remained and escaped to Nagore. From there he went to Medta and then to Tonk. Where could he go? Where would he be safe? Should he leave for Pakistan as well? The question haunted him. But somehow, he could not bring himself to take that step. So many whom he admired had not left. The famous poet Josh had stayed on. So had the beautiful Suraiya. How could he leave?

With time, everything that could fetch in a little money was sold. Yet there was no employment, no work in sight. At that time it was almost impossible for a Muslim to get a job. Besides Qurban bhai was not equipped to earn a living. He did not possess even the simplest of skills. His education too was incomplete. When at last he did get a job as an accountant in a shop his honesty and sincerity were distinct disadvantages. He was viewed with suspicion by Hindus and Muslims alike.

If he associated with the Hindus they treated him

as an outsider. And if he mingled with the Muslims he felt suffocated by the religious fervour of the various leagues. He could never regain the privileged position that he had once enjoyed. Unable to hold a steady job, his status in life kept falling. From a labourer he became a coolie ... and finally, he became humane. The force of circumstance taught him several new trades. He repaired punctured bicycle tyres, soldered tin cans, fixed locks, umbrellas and lanterns, dyed clothes, carved ivory bangles. And all the while he kept moving from one town to another. Whatever work he took up, it slowly slipped out of his hand. Now it was technology and not communalism that was the threat. Tossed about in this manner he finally reached our kasba. An elderly Muslim lent him fifty rupees. A small stock of rice and pulses, matches, bidis-cigarettes ... With these he started a shop. What do I say and how do I say it? The story of one man's struggle against overwhelming odds cannot be summed up neatly in a few words. It would not only be unfair but an impertinence.

But the story I am about to relate is an altogether different one.

Soon the grocery shop began making a small profit. It was more than enough to meet the simple requirements of Qurban bhai and his wife.

Their children were dead. There was no one to spend the extra money on.

So why not subscribe to magazines and newspapers? The idea appealed to Qurban bhai. He put it into practice. Whenever he was informed of the arrival of a magazine, by VPP or book post, he would go to the post office to fetch it. He would handle it with great care and read it from cover to cover. He would read it again and again. Like a starving man who had been served a feast. The love of poetry, literature, the arts, was still strong in him. And so he bought magazines, read them and preserved them.

It soon became clear to everyone that he was no ordinary shopkeeper.

His good breeding showed. He did not lie or cheat. He was always courteous. And ever willing to help anyone in need.

With time, he earned the respect of the entire kasba. Many respectable men began to frequent his shop. Qurban bhai would invite them to a cup of tea and they would discuss Ghalib's poetry.

Soon Qurban bhai's shop became a regular meeting point for the intellectuals of the kasba. Lecturers, teachers, writers and journalists would gather there every evening and the place would resound with their arguments and their laughter. Qurban bhai would call for tea, spread a mat on the floor and recite a couplet or two. Shopkeeping and discussions spiked with laughter would proceed side by side. Every now and then Qurban bhai would request one or the other of the gathering to wrap a handful of chillis or salt in a piece of paper, or to make out a bill for items purchased. It was not unusual to see a lecturer of English literature stand on the roadside and peel garlic. Or a newspaper editor squat on the floor and take multani mitti out of a sack.

Associating with us brought about a distinct change in Qurban bhai. He became aware of his literary bent of mind. He taught us Urdu. We rearranged his library, which had grown considerably by now. We had the journals bound and made extensive use of that library. We even convinced Qurban bhai to accompany us to mushairas and other cultural events. We introduced him to magazines and newspapers that he had never heard of, to writers he had only dreamt of, to poetry that had long ago bid farewell to romantic images of love and intoxication, to revolutionary political ideologies that he had only been vaguely aware of. In this process of brainwashing Qurban bhai, we rid him of all the obsolete notions about religion that had cluttered his thinking. We got him addicted to reading the newspaper in a way no one had done before. There were other changes in Qurban bhai. He began to take a weekly off.

He would join us for after-dinner walks. Instead of brooding over the past, he began to think of the future with growing optimism. In our company he regained a certain youthfulness. He took on all our habits.

And every evening he waited for us to appear at his shop. If, for some reason we could not keep the appointment, he would arrive at our homes.

We gained nothing from Qurban bhai's respectability. But for him, keeping company with us badly tarnished his image. The time he had spent earlier with Latif Sahab, Haji Sahab, Imam bhai and others was now spent with us. Then he used to read namaaz on Fridays. Now that too came to an end. Though he continued the practice of giving donations to the local madarasa, he was rebuked by members of his community for attending the occasional local political rallies and conferences. It was dangerous for him, they said. "Politics is not for us. Eat your food quietly and think of Allah. If you want to live in peace then don't get into all this. Not only will you get into trouble, you will drag us in, too. Now that we have to live here ..." But we were immersed in our own concerns. None of us, not even Qurban bhai, was aware of the growing animosity among the religious leaders from the Imambara. Or of the gradual alienation from the community. We did not pay any attention to the sudden absence of the self-proclaimed "patriots" who had once been part of our group. Till finally that incident occurred, the incident that brings this story to its regrettable end. An end that leaves a bitter taste ...

That afternoon a man in a bullock cart entered the chowk and stopped in front of Qurban bhai's shop. There was nothing unusual about this. Villagers who came into the kasba would always park their carts in the chowk, unyoke the bullocks, give them fodder, and then go about their tasks. They would return only in the evening. But until that day no one had ever parked his cart right at the entrance of a shop. This particular man did just that. He placed the cart in such a way that the entrance to Qurban bhai's shop was completely blocked. In fact even Qurban bhai could not leave the shop.

Qurban bhai recognized the man as Vakil Ukhchand's ploughman. Qurban bhai knew that if the man went away now he would only return in the evening.

Qurban bhai requested him to move the cart to the side and to tie the bullocks elsewhere. The man ignored him. When Qurban bhai repeated his request, he only glanced at him and went on his way. Qurban bhai began to move the cart to the side. But the man grabbed him by his neck and began to abuse him. He snatched at Qurban bhai's spectacles and hit him. At that very instant Vakil Ukhchand, on his way from court, passed by and shouted, What happened Gomaya? Gomaya replied, He is hitting me. Ukhchand asked, Who? This miyan, answered Gomaya. Qurban bhai was stunned. By the time the words sank in he was deeply shaken. Stars danced before his eyes. He sat right there on the ground and held his head. Bitterness rose in his heart and stuck in his throat.

Years of accumulated tears threatened to gush out at once.

What was happening? ... Doesn't Gomaya know him? How had he become "miyan" from "Qurban bhai" in one moment? The respect he had acquired bit by bit over the years ... Every moment of every day had been a test by fire ... The respect and love he had collected ... Telling himself that even if he returned to Pakistan he wouldn't get his old status back ... Whatever it was, however it was, it was fine here ... Allah can see everything ... Let Josh go, and Suraiya ... Let friends forget ... and business be lost ... Let the two havelis fall into the hands of lying cheats ... Let the graves of his two brothers go uncared for ... Let dreams be buried ... Perhaps his day will come too ... Be patient till then. At what price had he managed to feel a sense of belonging ... A little security ... A little confidence ... The little ease he had found ... He had thought of it as great wealth ... And now this. Everything was blown apart in one breath. One uncouth man – but who was uncouth, the ploughman or he himself? That I would become "miyan" from "Qurban bhai" in a moment – I had never considered it. Why? I have lived by hard work. Even then I am considered a burden. Why have I never recognized this? If I had gone to Pakistan ... I could have borne a million troubles ... at least I wouldn't have had to hear such an insult! To hell with such a life!

Allah! Ya Allah!

Vakil Ukhchand consoled Gomaya and took him away. He left the cart there. The neighbours took care of Qurban bhai. His jaw was hurt and he was frothing at the mouth. Some people removed the cart and the bullocks. They helped him lie on the platform, fanned him and sprinkled water on his face. They even cursed Vakil Ukhchand and tried to cheer up Qurban bhai. How were they to know how completely heartbroken Qurban bhai was?

All these years he had not allowed this pain to surface. Who can see the hurt that lies in one's heart?

People gathered together. The news spread through the entire town. As soon as we heard, we went there too. Scores of people had got together and the talk grew like fire. After much conferring it was decided that such insolence should not be tolerated in silence. They would report to the police. So a group trooped into the police station. On the way, several people dropped out under one pretext or other. By the time we reached the police station only Qurban bhai and a few of us were left. The inspector was not in. He had just gone out on his motorcycle. The constable was there. He refused to take down the complaint. And why not?

Vakil Ukhchand had already made a telephone call to the constable. Vakil Ukhchand was the secretary of the ruling party. Who was Qurban bhai? Who were we?

We pleaded for half an hour and waited for the inspector for an hour and a half and then went away disconsolate. We would return in the evening. No one came with us that evening. Qurban bhai did not show any enthusiasm. He appeared completely engrossed in running his shop and had no time to even talk to us.

We too remained distant from Qurban bhai. The incident was trivial. But what about the constable? Anyone in Qurban bhai's place wouldn't want to get involved with the police. He would choose to ignore the incident, forget it as a foolish act of an uncouth man. And what of us? We ... we felt that our friend had been attacked and we had been unable to do anything. We hadn't been able to help him in anyway. But we also felt that if we appeared too concerned, things would get more difficult for Qurban bhai. And we would still not be able to help. Also the realization had dawned that despite what had occurred, it was useless expecting assistance from the police. We could only deal with this issue at a political level, for which we would require to increase our strength as soon as possible.

These were only excuses. The truth was that we had deserted Qurban bhai. Perhaps we couldn't share his problems. But we should have made the attempt.

For several days there was no boisterous crowd at Qurban bhai's shop like there used to be. Qurban bhai remained morose, spoke little and whenever he saw us, busied himself with work in the shop. He was smouldering, suffocating, but refused to open up. We didn't help either. One day I reached his shop and heard him say to someone, What do you teach in history? You say the Partition *took* place! No, it is still taking place, right now ... but when he saw me, he fell silent and went about his work.

Partition

This story does not have a pleasant end. I wish you did not have to read it. If you do read it, think. Could there have been another ending? A better end? If so, how?

There is only this to say now. Many days later I was passing through Azad Chowk. It has since been renamed Sanjay Chowk. It was Friday. I saw Latif bhai in front of Qurban bhai's shop. Qurban bhai was locking up the shop. He was wearing a cap. Then the two men walked towards the masjid.

The
BLUE LIGHT
VAIKOM MUHAMMAD BASHEER

translated from Malayalam by C P A Vasudevan

I have had many unusual experiences in my life. The incident of the Blue Light is one such. Rather than call it an amazing experience, I should describe it as a bubble of mystery, which I have tried to prick with the pin of scientific enquiry, but have not been able to. Maybe you can even analyze and explain it.

I refer to it as an amazing experience because ... well, what else can I call it?

This is what happened.

The exact date is of no consequence really. It was the time when I was house hunting every other day, because I never seemed to find a room or house I really liked. The place I was living in had so many faults, but who could I complain to? "Don't like it? Then leave it!" is what I'd probably be told. Leave and go where? So I stayed, unwillingly, reluctantly, till it became unbearable. Then the search would begin once more. I was fed up. How many houses, how many rooms, had I lived in, and hated. It wasn't anybody's fault. I didn't like the place, so I moved out. Someone else who liked it, moved in. That's the way it is, I suppose, with all rented houses. But these days, houses tolet are in short supply. And the rents! What you could have got for ten is not available for even sixty today. Anyway ...

I was wandering around on my quest for a dwelling

when suddenly, there it was – a house, with an ancient signboard saying, HOUSE TOLET. It was a small, two-storey bungalow, standing beside the public road, far away from the bustle and the noise of the town, but within municipal limits. I liked it instantly. It was an old house, rather dilapidated and neglected. I didn't care. It was good enough to live in. Two rooms and a portico above, four rooms below, bathroom and kitchen, water connections, but no electricity. Just outside the kitchen was an old well with a stone parapet around it. The toilet stood in one corner of the compound. There were lots of trees. A compound wall enclosed the whole place. Fortunately there were no other buildings nearby.

I wondered why no one had grabbed it yet. It was like a beautiful woman, I thought, one you would want to shield from public view or hide behind a purdah. I was excited, and also afraid I might lose it. So I ran around trying to collect money for the advance. I borrowed enough to pay two months' rent, took the keys and quickly moved in, occupying the upper floor. The same day, I bought a hurricane lantern and some kerosene oil.

A great deal of garbage had accumulated all over the house. I cleaned the whole place myself, sweeping and mopping the rooms upstairs, the ones on the ground floor, the kitchen, the bathroom. What a lot of dust and rubbish! I went over it all a second time, thoroughly scrubbing the floor. That done, I had a bath. I felt very pleased. In this state of mind I went and sat on the parapet of the old well. How delightful this place was! Here I could sit and dream. Or run about the compound. I would plant a garden in front, roses mostly, and some jasmine. Should I hire a cook? No, that would be a headache. I could go out after a bath for my morning tea and bring some back in my thermos flask. Lunch would be at a restaurant. Perhaps they would agree to send my dinner home. I also had to meet the postman, tell him my new address and warn him not to give it to anyone. I could look forward to some lovely nights of solitude. Days too. I could write and write and write.

All these thoughts were racing through my mind as I sat there, gazing into the well. It was so overgrown with weeds that you couldn't tell if there was any water in it. Without thinking, I picked up a stone and dropped it into the depths. Bhloom! it went. Yes, there was water in the well.

I was feeling a little tired. I had not slept a wink the previous night because so many things had to be done. First, I had to settle my account at the eating house. Then meet the landlord and tell him I was moving out. After that, I had to pack. I bundled up my folding canvas cot, carefully put away my gramophone and records and tied them firmly together. Then I got my trunks, easy chair, shelf and all my belongings ready for transport. At the crack of dawn I had brought them to my new house.

I looked at my watch. Eleven o'clock. I was hungry, so I decided to go and find an eating place. I locked the front door, put the key in my pocket and shut the gate. As I stepped out on to the road, I thought to myself, With whose song, with which record, shall I inaugurate my new residence tonight? I have over a hundred records in English, Arabic, Hindi, Urdu, Tamil and Bangla. None, as you can see, in Malayalam. We do have talented Malayali singers and their records are available, but the compositions are not very good. A few new composers are coming up. I must buy some of their work. But tonight, whose song shall I play – Pankaj Mullick, Dilip Kumar Roy, Saigal, Bing Crosby, Paul Robeson, Abdul Karim Khan, Kanan Devi, Kumari Manju Dasgupta, Khurshid, Juthika Ray, M S Subbulakshmi ... Finally one comes to mind, *Door desh ka rahnewala aayaa* – "The man from a distant land has arrived." Who had sung that song? A man or a woman? Never mind. I would find out later.

Just then I met the postman. I told him of my change of residence. When he heard the new address, he was shocked.

"Ayyo saar! An unnatural death took place in that house. No one can live there. That is why it has been vacant for so long," he exclaimed. I was a bit rattled.

"What unnatural death?" I asked, taking hold of myself.

"You know that well in the compound? Someone jumped into it and died. Since then, the place has been haunted. Many people tried living there, but they found the doors kept banging at night and water taps were mysteriously opened."

Doors bang? Taps open by themselves? Strange. I recalled noticing that the taps had locks on them. The owner had told me it was to prevent trespassers from jumping the walls for a free bath. It had not occurred to me to ask why the tap inside the bathroom had a lock on it too. The postman went on, "It catches you by the throat, saar! Didn't anyone tell you all this?"

A fine dilemma I was in. I had paid two months' rent in advance and now ...

I put on a brave face. "That's all right. I only need one of my mantrams. You just make sure my letters are sent here."

Although I said this quite bravely, I am not really a brave man. But I'm not a coward either. I just fear all those things that most people are afraid of. Very well, let us say I am a coward for I do not go seeking unusual experiences. But if one comes unsought? What would happen? What should I do in this situation? As I walked along, my stride grew slower.

I entered a restaurant and ordered a cup of tea. My appetite for a proper meal had been replaced by a burning in the pit of my stomach. I spoke to the owner about sending my meals to the house. He saw the address and said, "I will send all your daytime meals. But at night, none of my boys will agree to go there. A woman jumped to her death in that well. She may still be hanging around." He looked at me again. "Aren't you afraid of ghosts, saar?"

"No. I'm not," I replied casually. "I have my mantram."

I kept talking about this mantram. What mantram? I didn't know either.

Hearing that the ghost was a woman, half my fear had evaporated and I was somewhat reassured. She must have some traces of tenderness still left in her, I told myself.

I had my tea, made arrangements for my food and then walked to the bank nearby where a couple of my friends were employed as clerks. I told them of my predicament and they promptly berated me.

"That was a very foolish thing to do. Couldn't you have asked us before you took the house? We would have advised you. The place is haunted. And it is men who are attacked by the ghost," they said.

So, it is men she hates.

"Who knew all this at that time? Anyway, why did the woman jump into the well?"

"Love. All for love," one of them said. "Bhargavi was her name. She was twenty one years old, had just finished her BA and had fallen passionately in love with this man. But the fellow went and married someone else. On his wedding night Bhargavi jumped into the well and died."

So that is why she hates men.

By this time most of my fear had gone.

Confidently, I told them, "Bhargavi won't bother me."

"Why won't she bother you?"

"My mantram, my mantram."

"We shall see. Soon you will be screaming for help."

I chose not to reply.

A little later I returned to the house. I opened the doors and windows. Then I went out to the well and called out softly, "Bhargavikutty!" After a few moments, I began …

"Bhargavikutty, we don't know each other. Let me tell you about myself. I am the new tenant here. I consider myself a very decent man. A confirmed bachelor. You know, Bhargavikutty, I have heard people make complaints about you. You won't let anyone live here in peace … You bang doors in the middle of the night. You open up the water taps. You put your hands around men's throats and strangle them … That's what I've heard. Now tell me, Bhargavikutty, what do you want me to do? I have paid two months' rent in advance, and I can't afford to let it go. I don't have pots of money.

The Blue Light

Besides, I like this house of yours very much. It is your own house, isn't it?

"I want to work here in peace and quiet. I write stories, Bhargavikutty. Tell me, do you like stories? If you do, I shall read all my stories out to you ... We have no quarrel with each other, do we? There is no reason for any. Oh yes! That stone I threw into the well. That was quite thoughtless of me. Forgive me. It will not happen again. Bhargavikutty, do you like music? I have a fine gramophone and a couple of hundred first class records."

I stopped. Who was I talking to? This well, with its gaping mouth, waiting to swallow anything that is thrown into it? The trees? The house, the air, the sky, the world ... to whom? Or is it to my own troubled mind? No, I said. It is to an abstraction that I speak. To Bhargavi, whom I have never seen. A young woman of twenty one. She loved a man. Dreamt of living as his wife, his lifetime companion. That dream remained a dream. Despair seized her. And disgrace ...

"Bhargavikutty," I said, "You need not have done this. Don't think I am criticizing you. True, the man you cared for did not love you. He married another. Your life was full of bitterness. But you must forget the past. For you, there will never be another disappointment.

"I am not finding fault with you, Bhargavikutty, but tell me honestly, did you die for the sake of love? Love is the Golden Dawn of Eternal Life. You didn't know much about that did you, you foolish girl? At least that's what your animosity to all men proves. Let us say, for argument's sake, you loved a man. He wronged you. Even so, is it right to see all men in the same light?

Had you lived longer, had you not taken your own life, you would have found that you were mistaken. There would have been another who loved you, who called you his goddess and worshipped you. But as I said earlier, you will never have such an experience. For you history will not be repeated ... Bhargavikutty, how will I ever get to know your story?"

I paused for a while. Then in a placating tone I continued, "Anyway, you must not trouble me, Bhargavikutty. This is not an order, it is only an entreaty. If you were to strangle me tonight, no one would come looking for revenge. Not that such a thing as revenge is possible in your case! What I mean is, there is no one to do it. You know why? Because I have no one to call my own.

"I hope you understand, now that you know everything. Both of us have to live here. Yes. I propose to stay. In the eyes of the law, this house, this well, they are all in my possession. But ignore that. We are going to share it. You may use all the rooms downstairs and the well. The kitchen and bathroom, we'll go fifty-fifty. Do you approve of the arrangement?"

I waited for an answer. Nothing happened. But I felt a sense of relief.

Night fell. After a meal at the restaurant I came home with my thermos full of tea. I lit the lantern by the light of my torch. The room was bathed in yellow light. I went downstairs. It was dark. I opened the windows, and stood there for a long time. Then through the kitchen I went to the well, intending to lock up the taps. But I changed my mind.

Coming inside, I shut and bolted the door, climbed

...irs to my room and poured myself some tea. I lit a ...nd sat in the easy chair, preparing myself to start ...ng. I felt someone was standing behind my chair.

"I do not like people peering over my shoulder when I write, Bhargavikutty," I said, and turned around.

There was no one there.

The mood to write was lost. Instead, I felt a strange restlessness, and began to pace up and down. Outside, the air was still. Not a leaf stirred. I glanced out of the window and suddenly, for the briefest moment I saw a light. Blue? Red? Yellow? I don't really know. It was only for a moment. Had I seen it, or was it my imagination? I wondered. But you can't imagine something like that. Must have been a firefly I saw.

I stood by the window for some time. Nothing happened. I tried to read but could not concentrate. I thought I would play one of my records. I lit the lantern again, opened the gramophone, fitted a new needle, wound it up. The world was silent, but there was a humming sound in my ears. Was I scared? A strange feeling crawled over my back. This silence was oppressive. I needed to shatter it into a million fragments. Who would do that for me? Which song would it be? After a brief search I picked out a record of the Black American singer, Paul Robeson. His deep baritone sang out, *Joshua fight the battle of Jericho*.

After that it was Pankaj Mullick with *Tu dar na zara bhi* – Do not be even a little afraid ... Then the enchanting *Katrinilay varum geetam* – wafting on the breeze comes the song, by M S Subbulakshmi. Slowly, I began to feel at peace with myself. I had Saigal himself sing in that gentle, comforting voice of his, *So jaa rajakumari, so jaa* – Go to sleep, my princess, go to sleep.

"That's all for now, Bhargavikutty. Tomorrow there will be more." I called out, as I closed the gramophone, lit a bidi, extinguished the light and lay down. By my side were the torch and my watch. The door to the portico was shut.

It was around ten o'clock. There was silence all around, but for the ticking of the watch. I lay with my ears strained. There was no fear in my mind, only a sort of calm watchfulness. It was a familiar feeling. I had known it in different places, in the different lands that I had travelled, during the twenty odd years of my solitary existence. I have had experiences whose meaning I have never been able to comprehend. My thoughts kept shuttling between the past and present. But at the back of my mind I was waiting. Is the door about to bang? Was that the sound of water flowing? Will her hands ... Such thoughts kept me awake until three in the morning. All this while I heard nothing, felt nothing, experienced nothing. Not even dreams.

It was nine in the morning when I woke up. Nothing had happened!

"Good morning, Bhargavikutty!" I called out cheerily. "Many thanks! Now I know you are being maligned. But let them say whatever they want, eh?"

Many days and nights went by. Bhargavi was always on my mind – her mother, father, brothers, sisters – whose stories I did not yet know. Most nights I wrote. And when I grew tired of writing, I played my records. Before each record I would announce the name of the singer and explain the meaning of the song, "Listen. This is by the great Bengali singer, Pankaj

Mullick. It is a sad song about old times. Listen carefully."

Guzar gayaa won zamaanaa, kaise, kaise.

Or, "This is Bing Crosby's *In the Moonlight* which means ... Oh, forgive me. I forgot you have a BA degree."

And so I would carry on this conversation, all by myself.

Two months and a half went by. During this time. I had completed a short novel. I had even laid out a garden and announced that when the flowers came, they would all be Bhargavikutty's. My friends visited me, and sometimes they even spent the night at my house. On such occasions, before going to bed I would quietly slip downstairs and speak into the darkness.

"Listen, Bhargavikutty. My friends are here tonight. Don't strangle them. If something like that happens, the police will come and take me away. So take care. Good night!"

Whenever I went out, I would tell her, "Bhargavikutty, look after the house. If a thief breaks in, feel free to strangle him. Only don't leave the body here. Carry it off and throw it three miles away. Otherwise we'll be in trouble." If I returned home late after a night show I would always call out from the front door, "It's only me, Bhargavikutty!"

All this, let me admit, came out of the initial excitement and novelty of living in a haunted house. As the days wore on, however, Bhargavi faded from memory. There were no more long monologues. Only an occasional mental glance in her direction.

Let me explain why this happened. From the beginning of the human race, countless men and women have died on this earth, have they not? All of them have dissolved in the waters or gone up in smoke or turned to dust – to rejoin the earth in one form or another. We all know that. In my mind, Bhargavi too had entered that category of beings. She had lapsed into memory.

That's when it happened.

I had been working on a story, a very powerful, emotional one, from nine o'clock in the night. I was writing furiously, when I noticed the light was getting dim. I picked up the lantern and shook it gently. No oil. I was too deeply involved with the story to stop now. I thought that I would write another page at least. I had done it before, writing in the fading light. So I raised the wick and continued. The light faded again. Up went the wick a second time, and a third, all four inches of it, until it turned into a mere glow. I switched on the torch, turned the wick of the lantern all the way down and needless to say, the light went out. What could I do now? I had to have some oil for the lantern. It was after ten o'clock. Where could I get kerosene oil at this time of night? Ah yes! My bank friends used a kerosene stove. I could borrow some from them.

With torch and bottle, I left the room, shut and locked the door behind me, went down the stairs, locked the front door and walked to the gate. Closing it behind me, I strode down the empty road. It was cloudy but there was a little moonlight. I walked fast.

When I reached the bank building, I called out to one of my friends. He came down and opened a side gate. I entered the compound, went to the rear of the building and climbed the stairs. I found three of them playing a game of cards. When I asked for the oil, they laughed.

"Why didn't you send your girlfriend Bhargavi?

Have you finished writing her story?"

I did not reply. But in my mind I resolved that I would, indeed, write it. As one of my friends started to pour the oil out of his stove into my bottle, it began to rain.

"Now you will have to lend me an umbrella as well," I said.

"Umbrella? We don't have even a piece of an umbrella. Why don't you join in the game? You can go when it stops raining."

I sat down. Because of my carelessness my partner and I had to perform three salaams in forfeits. My mind was still on the story, and the cards did not get the attention they deserved.

Around one o'clock it stopped raining. I finished the game, picked up my torch and bottle and got ready to leave. My friends prepared to go to bed. When I reached the road they turned their lights off.

Not a soul stirred. The street was dark. In the dull moonlight, the whole world lay hidden behind an indistinct veil of mystery. I walked quickly in the direction of my house. What thoughts raced through my mind at that time, I do not know. Flashing my torch, I trod the silent, deserted road. Not a single living creature crossed my path.

Reaching the house, I opened the gate, walked up to the front door, entered it and bolted it behind me. There was no reason to suspect that anything unusual had happened. And yet, for no special reason, my mind was filled with a strange melancholy. Normally, I laugh easily but find it impossible to shed tears. Instead, a kind of compassion overcomes me. It came to me then and I felt that I must weep. In that emotional frame of mind I went up the stairs. A strange sight met my eyes.

When I had left the house my lantern had gone out for want of oil. The room lay in darkness. Since then, two or three hours had passed. It had also rained.

Now when I returned, I could see a light in the room through the crack in the door. It was a brilliant light that my eyes saw and my subconscious registered. My rational, conscious mind had not taken note of it yet. As usual, I took the key out of my pocket and flashed my torch on the lock. It shone like silver and it seemed to smile at me. I opened the door. Every fibre of my being was startled into awareness. A tremor shook my body. But it was not in fear that I shivered. It was a mixture of love and compassion. I stood there, still, speechless. I felt hot. I perspired. I wanted to cry.

The room, the white walls, everything, glowed in a blue light. A light from the lantern, burning with a two-inch tongue of blue flame.

Who had lit the lantern? Where had that blue light come from?

"The Blue Light" was first translated and published by Katha in *Visions Revisions 1* in May 1995

The
PURPLE HAZE

VASUDHA MANE

translated from Marathi by the Author

The fat headmistress entered the classroom. As usual, her glasses were perched on her nose and she held a cane in her hand. The thirty children in class four had the usual feeling. Their hearts stopped beating.

They stood up to greet the headmistress. She marched straight up to the class teacher, tiny Mrs Karpe, who looked even smaller beside her.

"Inspection after eight days," the headmistress announced. "Is everything ready?"

"Yes," Mrs Karpe replied meekly.

"Make sure that all the girls bring their needlework," she boomed looking pointedly at me. And then she marched out of the classroom.

The class returned to its noisy self. Before this interruption, I had been thinking about the doll I had seen long ago, in Belgaum. Mrs Shevde had brought it over to the school to show it to us. The doll was so beautiful, I just couldn't forget it, specially the doll's dress.

It was made of extremely fine material. I wanted to tell my friend Prema about it but the thought of needlework pushed everything else out of my mind.

"Vasanthi! Stand up!" That was Mrs Karpe. "Don't forget to bring your needlework tomorrow, understand?"

"Yes," I said. Though I did not quite know why I

said it. I knew I would not be able to get any cloth for the needlework.

Evening came and I was back home. Aai had not yet returned from her school. I lit the fire in the kitchen and went to Dabholkar kaki's to fetch the milk vessel. She had already boiled the milk.

"Why did you?" I asked. "I would have done it myself."

Kaki smiled. "Silly child," she said. "You had tea? I have made some."

"Nai, nai Kaki!" I replied hastily and ran back with the milk. To make tea of course.

The chulha burned brightly, furiously as a matter of fact. I reduced its fury. And then put the water to boil.

Aai should be coming any moment. She should have tea. She was teaching in an English High School. PT. Gave tuitions too, in the mornings, from seven thirty to nine thirty. She had to, to keep the three of us going. We all knew about Baba. From the newspapers, mainly. He was in jail. Ever since Subhas Babu disappeared from the surface of the earth.

Even before he went to jail Baba was never at home. But whenever he came, it was a festival for us. Once he came with his long, dirty woollen coat. His method of drycleaning was simple, without fuss. He simply beat the coat against the wall to rid it of all the dust it had collected. Drycleaning over, he told Aai to get him something to eat. He went out and came back after fifteen days. Must have eaten somewhere else.

I have learnt one lesson rather well. When someone comes home tired after a day's work, don't pester him or her with any demand.

But it was all right to practise making the demand. For one yard of cloth. The demand would be addressed to Aai. Of course I was minding the chulha all the while.

Pramila and Shrikant were there. I gave them each a cup of tea and sent them out to play.

I was about to drink my tea when I heard Aai's footsteps.

"Tea is ready!" I called out even before she entered, very pleased with my strategy.

"Shabash!" Aai said.

It made me quite hopeful. I waited for Aai to finish her tea before launching the attack.

"Inspection in eight days," I said casually, my back to her. I was washing up, as a preliminary.

"I know," Aai said. "Mrs Chiplunkar is coming."

"How do you know?" I was astonished. Aai knew everything! She smiled.

"She's very strict ... that's what they say." I was making conversation.

Aai was silent. She was sitting, leaning against the wall, her legs stretched out before her. Her eyes were closed. Aai had a sharp nose. It seemed to pierce right through me.

I gathered up all the courage I had. "The teacher asked me to bring my needlework for the inspection," I said.

"Put the rice to boil, will you?" Aai had probably not heard about the needlework, nor about the inspection.

I did not have the courage to pursue the conversation further. I stuffed another log into the mouth of the chulha and put the rice vessel on.

I got up and brought the pillow, the only one in

the house, gave it to Aai and told her to rest.

"Where are Shri and Pammi?" she asked stretching out. "Tell them to come in. They've played enough. Let them start with the tables."

It had become dark. I got busy with the lantern, striking matchstick after matchstick. It was no use. Then I lifted up the dome and shook it. No oil. Not in the lantern. Not at home either.

"No oil," I said to Aai.

"No oil?" Aai was fully rested now. "Well, we will have the purple haze then ..."

Our house had been partitioned recently. Between us and our tenants.

Without them we would not have been able to manage, really. The partition was made of matting. So when the tenants lit the lantern in the evening, we got part of the light too. It was a bright light, a really bright shadow, actually. The shadow of life. The purple haze ... our surprise diwali ... the diwali we celebrated once a fortnight, at least. The purple haze. We had the haze this evening too. The kitchen was aglow. The chulha saw to it.

We had our food. Washing up was my job. Shri and Pammi went to sleep early. I was pressing Aai's tired feet.

"I need a yard of cloth," I said once again. "It is not expensive, really. Only twelve annas a yard."

Aai was silent. For a while. Finally she spoke, very, very softly, "Vasanthi, child, not this month. Next month maybe. I'll come and speak to your teacher."

"The inspection?" I could bring out no other word.

Aai sat up. I could see her face, blurred, but visible. The tenant's lantern helped me see it.

"Don't worry, child. I'm there, aren't I. I'll see your Inspectress too ..." After a short pause, she took a deep breath and whispered, "These days will pass, I'm sure of it. Things have to change after all ..." Then her voice grew a little louder. "Not today, maybe, but some day we will be free. And when the country is free, your father too will be free ... out of jail." Now Aai's voice blurred too. She continued, "The purple haze cannot last for ever. It has to go ..."

"We will be free, God willing ..." I said it too.

Suddenly, Aai flared up. "God willing? What has God to do with it? So many of our people are languishing in jails, so many children are waiting for their fathers to return ... All this can't be for nothing! We *will* be free one day! And then there will be everything for everyone."

Aai's words made me feel very happy. I hugged her and went off to sleep. Aai was always like that. A little on the loud side whenever under stress, but ...

She gave speeches, I believe, before I was born. And when she made a speech she had no fear, none at all.

The purple haze bathed the needlework, the Inspectress, everything in its purple glory.

But the class teacher did not stop making her demand. For a yard of cloth.

Not that I asked Aai again.

We were preparing for the welcome ceremony. I was going to be the leader of the welcome group. So the teacher stopped pestering me. Aai was busy with her school. The inspection was to be held in her school too, so she was late every evening. When she came home, we exchanged notes – what her school was doing for their inspection, and what we were doing for ours.

The Great Day came. I had decided to get up before Aai, have a bath and touch her feet. When I opened my eyes, Aai was ready to leave for work. No time even for a quick namaskar. "Blessings can be taken once the work is done," she used to say.

I had my bath. The previous night I had put my one good yellow frock under my pillow. For it to iron itself out. As I slipped it on, I heard that fatal sound. A rip! I was in tears. But I had no time. I looked for something whole to wear. I rummaged through all the trunks.

They were full. Of torn clothes. But I finally did see something that was still whole. A black blouse. With a gold border. I was pleased. I looked over it carefully. It was absolutely all right, except for the buttons. There was not a single button on the blouse. I put it on over the frock with the tear. Then I rushed to Dabholkar kaki and asked her to stitch up the blouse in front.

All this took a lot of time. I ran as fast as I could to school.

It seemed like it was the auspicious muhurta of a wedding. The school was all decked up. Mango leaves had been strung to decorate the main gate. The fragrance of agarbattis, supplied generously for the occasion, filled the classrooms.

Place the plantain leaves for the food, Vasanthi! In a straight row, please! The headmistress did not say that, of course, but she might as well have.

The class teacher spotted me in all the hectic activity. "Late again as usual," she said. She had no time to say anything else.

Kasturi, Pramodini, Prema, Shevanti ... the whole lot gathered round me. To admire my blouse.

"Real zari?" Prema wanted to know, as she felt the border. I was about to tell them the truth.

"Girls for the welcome song, this way please!" That was the headmistress's booming voice

I couldn't tell the whole truth about the blouse. The ceremony had started.

I tried to look at the Inspectress. She looked quite happy. Cheerful.

Everything will be all right, I told myself.

The welcome song over, we dispersed into our classrooms. The inspection began. My class was the first target. Not just that. Needlework was the bull's eye.

All the girls had displayed their needlework on their desks. All the girls except me, that is. I had nothing to display.

I could see two feet beneath the black border of a nine yard saree. They were approaching my desk. My breath stuck in my throat.

My eyes threatened to fill.

"What's your name? Stand up!" the words were familiar, but the tone was different, unknown.

"Vasanthi Deshpande," I blurted out, standing up.

"Needlework?" The question was familiar. Not the voice that asked it.

I don't have any, I gestured, shaking my head.

"Why not?" The question was again familiar. The voice remained strange.

"No money ..." I answered, my voice just above a whisper.

I marvelled at my tears. They had not left my eyes. I was ashamed of myself. If only I could melt away, melt away like ice.

"Can't afford it, can you? Can't afford plain cloth for needlework but can afford blouses with zari borders, hanh?" It was the same unfamiliar voice, rude now.

My fear, my sense of shame, everything vanished. I looked straight into her eyes. When I spoke it was my mother's voice that came out.

"You don't know what the zari border is hiding," I said. "It is the purple haze ... Some children have lots of purple haze in their lives! Do you know that? How dare you make fun of it!" Abruptly, I stopped.

And walked out of the classroom. I ran all the way home and cried and cried.

The whole afternoon was spent in cleaning the house.

I collected some flowers in the evening. I spread a mat on the ground and sat down weaving the flowers into a veni. I was so deeply engrossed in it that I did not see Aai and the visitor she had with her.

I looked up. Instinctively, I stood up. It was the Inspectress! She was staring hard at the zari border on my blouse. And then she spoke. "So this is the house with the purple haze!" she said slowly.

~JALEBiS~
AHMED NADEEM QASMI

translated from Urdu by Sufiya Pathan

It happened many years ago. I was in the fifth standard at the government school, Kambelpur, now called Atak. One day, I went to school with four rupees in my pocket to pay the school fees and the fund. When I got there I found that the teacher who collected the fees, Master Ghulam Mohammed, was on leave and so the fees would be collected the next day. All through day the four rupiya coins simply sat in my pocket, but once school got over and I was outside, they began to speak.

All right. Coins don't talk. They jingle or go khanak-khanak. But I'm telling you, that day they actually spoke! One rupiya said, "What are you thinking about? Those fresh, hot jalebis coming out of the kadhao in the shop over there, they're not coming out for nothing. Jalebis are meant to be eaten and only those with money in their pocket can eat them. And money isn't for nothing. Money is meant to be spent and only they spend it, who like jalebis."

"Look here you four rupiyas," I said to them, "I am a good boy. Don't misguide me or it won't be good for you. I get so much at home that I consider even looking at something in the bazaar a sin. Besides, you are my fees and fund money. If I spend you today then how shall I show my face to Master Ghulam Mohammed in school tomorrow and after that to Allah miyan at

Qayamat? You probably don't know it, but when Master Ghulam Mohammed gets angry and makes you stand on the bench, he simply forgets to let you sit till the last bell rings. So it's best you stop chewing at my ears like this and let me go home straight."

The rupiyas disliked what I'd just said so much that all of them began to speak at the same time. There was such a clamour that passersby in the bazaar stared, eyes wide with surprise, at me and my pocket. The rupiya of those days, the wretched thing, made so much more noise too! Finally, in a panic, I grabbed all four of them and held them tight in my fist and then they were silent.

After taking a few steps, I loosened my grip. Immediately the oldest rupiya said, "Here we are trying to tell you something for your own good and you try to strangle us instead. Tell me honestly now, don't you feel like eating those fresh, fresh, hot, hot jalebis? And then, if you do end up spending us today, won't you get the scholarship money tomorrow? Sweets with the fees money, fees with the scholarship money. End of story! Kissa khatm, paisa hazm."

"What you are saying isn't right," I replied, "But it isn't all that wrong either. Listen. Stop blabbering and let me think. I am not a common sort of boy."

"All right," said the oldest coin, "You're not a common sort of boy. But then, these jalebis are no common sort of jalebis either. They're crisp, fresh and full of sweet syrup."

My mouth watered, but I wasn't about to be swept away so easily. In school I was among the most promising students. In the fourth standard exams, I had even won

JALEBIS

a scholarship of four rupees a month. Besides, I came from a particularly well-to-do family, so I enjoyed considerable prestige. I'd never once been beaten so far. On the contrary, Masterji had got me to beat the other boys. For a child of such status to stand in the middle of the bazaar eating jalebis? No. It just wasn't right, I decided. I clenched the rupiyas in my fist and came home.

The rupiyas were so keen on being spent that day, they kept up their attempts at persuasion till their voices began to choke. When I reached home and sat on the bed, they began to speak. I went inside to have lunch, they began to shriek. Thoroughly fed up, I rushed out of the house barefoot and ran towards the bazaar. Terrified I was, but quickly I told the halwai to weigh a whole rupee worth of jalebis. His astonished look seemed to be asking me where I had the handcart in which I would carry all those jalebis. Those were inexpensive times. One rupee fetched far more jalebis than Rs 20 does nowadays. The halwai opened up a whole newspaper and heaped a pile of jalebis on it.

Just as I was gathering up the heap, in the distance I spotted our tanga. Chichajaan was returning from Court. I clutched the jalebis to my chest and ran into a gali. When I reached a safe corner I began to devour the jalebis. I ate so many ... so many ... jalebis that if anyone just pressed my stomach a little, jalebis would have popped out of my ears and nostrils.

Very quickly, boys from the entire neighbourhood assembled in the gali. By that time I was so pleased with my stomach full of jalebis that I got into the mood for some fun. I started handing out jalebis to the children around. Delighted, they ran off, jumping and screaming, into the galis. Soon a whole lot of other children appeared, probably having heard the good news from these kids. I dashed to the halwai and bought one more rupee's worth of jalebis, came back and stood on the chabutara of one of the houses, liberally distributing jalebis to the kids just like the Governor sahab used to distribute rice to the poor and needy on Independence day. By now there was a huge mob of children around me. The beggars too launched an assault! If children could be elected to the Assembly, my success would have been assured that day. Because one little signal from my jalebi-wielding hand and the mob would have been willing to kill and get killed for me. I bought jalebis with the remaining two rupees as well and distributed them. Then I washed my hands and mouth at the public tap and returned home, putting on such an innocent face, as if I hadn't even seen the hint of a jalebi all my life. Jalebis I had gobbled up easily enough, but digesting them became another matter. With every breath came a burp, and with every burp, the danger of bringing out a jalebi or two – the fear was killing me. At night I had to eat my dinner as well. If I hadn't eaten I would have been asked to explain why I did not want any food, and if had I pretended illness, the doctor would have been summoned and if the doctor, after feeling my pulse, had declared, Munna has devoured a mound of jalebis, I would simply die.

The result was that all night I lay, coiled up like a jalebi, suffering a stomach ache. Thank god I didn't have to eat all four rupees worth of jalebis by myself. Otherwise, as they say, when children speak, flowers shower from their mouths, but I would be the first child

Jalebis

in the world with whose every word a crisp, fried jalebi would come out.

Children don't have stomachs, they have digestion machines. My machine too kept working right through the night. In the morning, just like any other day I washed my face and like a virtuous student, with chalk and slate in hand, I headed for school. I knew I would get the previous month's scholarship money that day and once I'd paid my fees with that amount, the jalebis would be completely digested. But when I got to school I found out that the scholarship was going to be paid the following month. My head started to spin. I felt as if I was standing on my head and could not get back on to my feet again even if I tried.

Master Ghulam Mohammed announced that the fees would be taken during the recess. When the recess bell rang, I tucked my bag under my arm and left the school and simply followed my nose, walking on and on ... If no mountain or ocean blocked my path, I would have kept going till the earth ended and the sky began and once I got there I would say to Allah miyan, "Allah miyan, ab se hamari taubah! Bas, just this once save me. Order a farishta to pass by and drop just four rupees in my pocket. I promise I will use them only to pay my fees and not to eat jalebis."

I couldn't reach the point where the earth ended, but hanh, I definitely reached the spot where the Kambelpur railway station began. The elders had warned me never to cross the railway tracks. Fine. The elders had also warned me that one must never eat sweets with one's fees money. How did this instruction escape my mind that day? I don't know.

There was a shade-giving tree beside the railway tracks. I sat under it and wondered whether there could possibly be a more unfortunate child than me in this world! When the rupiyas had first created a racket in my pocket, the entire matter seemed so simple and straightforward. Eat jalebis with the fees money and then pay the fees with the scholarship money. I thought that two and two always added up to four and could never be five. How was I to know that sometimes it adds up to five as well. Had I known that I would get the scholarship the next month, I would have postponed my jalebi eating programme to the next month as well. Now for the crime of eating a few jalebis, for the first time in my life I was absent from school, and crouching in the shade of a tree in a deserted corner of the railway station. Sitting there under the tree, at first I felt like crying. Then I felt like laughing when it struck me that these tears I was shedding were not tears but drops of jalebi syrup. From the jalebis my thoughts went to the fees, and from fees to Master Ghulam Mohammed's cane, and from his cane I thought of God. I closed my eyes and with great intensity, began to pray.

"Allah miyan! I'm a very good boy. I have memorized the entire namaaz. I even know the last ten surats of the Quran by heart. If you wish I can recite the entire ayat-al-kursi for you just now. The need of your devoted servant is only the fees money that I ate jalebis with ... So all right, I admit I made a mistake. I didn't eat them all by myself though, I fed them to a whole lot of children too, but yes, it was a mistake. If I'd known the scholarship money would be given next month, I would neither have eaten them

Jalebis

nor fed them to the others. Now you do one thing, just put four rupees in my bag. If there's a paisa more than four rupees I will be very displeased with you. I promise if I ever eat sweets with my fees money again, then let a thief's punishment be my punishment. So, Allah miyan, just this once help me out. There is no shortage of anything in your treasury. Even our chaprasi takes a whole lot of money home every month, and Allahji, after all I am the nephew of a big officer. Won't you give me just four rupees?"

After the prayer I offered namaaz, recited the last ten surats, ayat-al-kursi, kalma-e-tayyab, in fact everything that I remembered. Then I blew over my bag saying Choo. When, after saying bismillah, I opened it, I realized that what they said was only too true – no one can erase what fate has decreed. Forget four rupees, there weren't even four paise in my bag. Just a few textbooks and notebooks. One pencil. One sharpener. One old Id card my Mamu had sent me last Id.

I felt like crying as loudly as I could, but then I remembered that school must have ended and the children must be on their way home. Tired and defeated, I got up from there and walked to the bazaar and waited for the school bell to ring, so that when the children came out I too would walk home with them as if I had come straight from school.

I didn't even realize that I was standing near the jalebiwala's shop. Suddenly, the halwai called out. "Kyon bhai, shall I weigh a rupee's worth? Don't want jalebis today?"

I felt like saying I won't eat your jalebis today but hanh, I'd sure like to roast your liver and eat that instead. But I wasn't feeling too well that day, so I simply moved away.

The next day I did the same thing. I got dressed and left home, went up to the school gate and then turned off to the railway station. Under the same tree I sat and began to say the same prayers. I repeatedly pleaded, Allah miyan! At least give it to me today. Today is the second day.

Then I said, "All right, come, let's play a game. I will go from here to that signal. You secretly place four rupees under this big rock. I will touch the signal and come back. What fun it will be if I pick up the rock and find four rupees underneath! So, are you ready? I am going towards the signal. One-two-three."

I went up to the signal and returned, smiling. But I could not find the courage to pick up the rock. What if the rupiyas were not there? But then, I thought, what if they were?

Finally, after saying bismillah, when I lifted up the rock, this long, hairy worm got up, and curling and twisting wriggled towards me. I screamed and ran away and once again touched the signal. Then, crawling on hands and knees, I reached the tree. I tried my best not to let my eyes stray towards the rock. But as I picked up my bag and was about to leave, I had to look once again at that rock, and do you know what I saw there? I saw Mr Worm coiled on it comfortably, staring at me.

I walked away thinking, Tomorrow I will do wazu, wear clean clothes and come here. From morning to noon I will keep reading the namaaz. If, even after that Allah doesn't give me four rupees, I will be forced to learn how to strike bargains or make deals with Him. After all, if my Allah won't give me my four rupees then who will? That day, when I returned home, apparently from school and actually from the railway station, I was caught. The report of my absence had reached home. It's useless to relate what happened after that.

Well, whatever happened, happened. But up to the seventh or eighth standard I kept wondering, if Allah miyan had sent me four rupees that day, what harm could it possibly have caused anyone? It was only later that I came to the conclusion that if Allah miyan were to provide all for the asking, then man would, even today, be living in nests in trees like vultures and crows and would not have learnt the art of making jalebis!

ARJUN
MAHASWETA DEVI

translated from Bangla by Mridula Nath Chakraborty

Aghrayan was almost over and the month of Poush was just round the corner. It was not cold enough yet for the sun's warmth to be welcome.

The ripe paddy crop in Bishal Mahato's farm had been harvested the previous day. All day, along with the harvesters and casual grain pickers, Ketu Shabar too had been collecting the leftover grains of paddy in the fields. Now, in foggy twilight, he needed a little liquor to warm him and to relax his aching body. The desire was sure to remain ungratified, but, he told himself, there was no harm in fantasizing.

His wife, Mohoni, was not with him. She came to the fields only when he was not around – Ketu was frequently in and out of jails. His offence – clearing the jungles for the paddy crop.

It was no use trying to reason with Ketu Shabar about this. Ram Haldar gave him the job and Ketu did it. Haldar collected the profits from the felled trees, and Ketu and others like him went to jail. But what could he do? All that mattered was the four pice at the end of the day – be it for chopping down a tree or chopping up a man. In fact, it might be easier to chop up a man! Why hadn't anyone asked him to do that? wondered Ketu. He might even earn four whole rupees that way! But he quickly corrected himself – I didn't mean it seriously, of course.

Ketu does not ever question his predicament. If you were born in the Shabar tribe of Purulia, you had to cut down the trees. And you had to go to jail. It could be no other way. If one Ketu was in jail, and something needed to be done, Haldar could always find another Ketu. Nothing lost – except that the woman in the house had to go looking for work.

The last time Ketu had been jailed for cutting down the trees of the Forest Department, Mohoni had gone out looking for work. And who knows what happened ... In spite of the inevitability of the situation, Ketu couldn't face the prospect of returning to an empty hut. No wonder the mind and the body demanded liquor. A little intoxication, a little oblivion ...

Lost in reverie, Ketu was suddenly confronted by Bishal Mahato. "I have some work for you," he said.

"Is it about the votes, babu?"

"No, no! I'm not worried about that. The people will have to elect whoever I nominate, won't they?"

"Hanh, babu."

"Well? What did Ram Haldar tell you?"

"The same thing that you said."

"And what was your reply?"

"Just what I told you."

"What kind of an answer is that?"

"I am just a fool, babu," said Ketu.

"Never mind. There is something I want you to do. Are you interested?"

Ram Haldar and Bishal Mahato belonged to different parties. But for Ketu and his companions, they were two of a kind. One had to appear dumb whenever they were around. Both these deities had to be pleased, if one were to make a living in this area. But who among them would dare to say "No" to these party members? Haldar and Mahato too knew that the Shabars were indispensable – they held the world record for jail terms, after all.

Now, Bishal Mahato had indeed managed to arouse Ketu's curiosity. Elections were around the corner. Bishal babu had been busy – attending meetings, giving speeches. So if the matter didn't concern votes, what could it possibly be? Whatever it was, it must be something dubious.

"You have to cut down the arjun tree," Bishal said.

"Why, babu?" Ketu was startled.

"Just do what I say."

"Please babu, I've just come out of jail, babu."

"If I wanted to send you back, would you be able to prevent it?" asked Bishal Mahato.

"No, babu."

"This is not like one of Ram Haldar's contracts. Only through his illegal operations do you land in jail. Who'd dare to arrest you if I ordered the removal of the tree from the main intersection at the government road?"

Ketu's mind went blank. He had never thought about it, but it was true. You worked for Ram Haldar and you promptly got caught. That meant another trip to the jail. But Bishal babu's word was law. He actually ran the country, you know! So, who would send you to jail if, under his instructions, the shade-giving tree no longer stood at the government road?

An idea flashed through Ketu's mind. "Babu, are you making a pucca road this time, to ensure the votes?

"Pucca road? Here? Ketu, you must be mad! It has

not happened in thirty years. And it won't happen now. No, I need the tree."

"A full-grown tree?"

"Yes, the whole arjun tree."

"And how would you transport it?"

"Ram babu's truck, what else."

It was as if the clear sky, the pure, cold, air and the Santoshi Ma bhajans blaring out on the cassette player were prompting Bishal Mahato to speak the truth.

It was that magical hour when earth bids farewell to the day and twilight disappears into the arms of night. The wind carried the smell of ripe paddy from the field of Bandihi. But Ketu was oblivious to all that. Mahato's request had stunned him. It was as if a huge stone had been placed on his chest. This is what Chandra Santhal must have felt when, during the harvest revolution, they had pinned him down with a half-maund measure. That weight ... Frightening.

Bishal Mahato and Ram Haldar belonged to two different parties. But only in word did they represent opposite camps. One conducted the Panchayat, the other ran the sawmill just outside the borders of the district. If one ordered the arjun to be cut down, the other happily provided the transport to carry it away.

Hai! The tree couldn't be saved. It was the only surviving relic of the Bandihi jungles from the Zamindari era. It still evoked memories of the past in the minds of Ketu and his friends.

When the jungles were not jungles in name only, the Shabars had been forest dwellers. Gone were those days when they scampered off like rabbit into its dark depths the moment they heard or saw a stranger approaching. Was that why they had been identified as Khedia Shabars, in the census records?

The elders of the tribe still revered the arjun tree. They believed that it was a manifestation of the divine. Now Ketu was to be responsible for its death!

"Yes, babu. I'll cut it down," Ketu Shabar said. He stretched out his hand for ten rupees.

What a strange evening this was. He was even given what he had asked for.

"Go, go drink," Mahato said. "You won't be able to manage the job on your own, so get all those just released from jail. I'll see to it that you are all taken care of."

Ram Haldar's business did not stop with one or two trees. First, he put up posters, "Save the Forests," then, vandalized the jungles. Hands that wielded the axe were rewarded with torches, wrist watches, gleaming radios, cassette players, cycles, and of course, unlimited quantities of liquor. Each according to his capacity and capability. But the fallout was that whether innocent or guilty, the Shabars were repeatedly persecuted by the Forest Department or the Police.

Mahato's offer was much more promising. Who else would offer them so much?

"Very well, I'm going to the town now. For a meeting ... I must get some posters. How on earth can one conduct a campaign without walls?"

"Get some for me too, babu."

"Why, do you have a wall to stick them on?"

"No, no, babu. I'll spread them out on the floor when I sleep. Then I won't feel the cold in my bones."

"All right, all right. See that you cut down the tree

in two or three days. I'll have it removed when I return."

"The arjun tree, babu?"

"Yes, yes, that one. Of course, it will be like the death of a mahapatra, a noble soul ..." the monkey-capped, sweater-clad Mahato muttered as he disappeared into the foggy darkness of the night.

Ketu was deep in thought. He went to look for his friends – Banamali, Diga and Pitambar – to see if they could offer a solution.

Since he was carrying liquor, they welcomed him warmly. All of them had wielded the axe. All of them were just out of jail. He who wields the axe goes to jail – that was the rule of the land. Just as it was understood that Ram Haldar would get palatial mansions built in Purulia and Bankura. That was fate. So what could they possibly do to change the order of things?

"Let me think," said Diga. Among them, Diga was treated with a little more respect. He had actually attended four whole days at the non-formal education centre! And learnt the alphabet too.

The four Shabars drowned themselves in thought and liquor. During festivals and weddings, they went around the arjun tree, beating their dhol-dhamsas. After a certain wish had been granted, the tribals made the ritual sacrifice of their hair and buried it under the tree for good luck. Hadn't Diga's father said that the tree had medicinal properties? Drunkenly, Pitambar exclaimed, "Even the Santhals come here during the Badhna Jagoran for the cow dance."

What a predicament! Cut the tree, you go to jail; don't cut the tree, you still get jailed. What is the Shabar to do? This prosperous village of Bandihi sits where once the jungle used to be. Now it falls under the jurisdiction of the Forest Department. But of course the Shabars don't have any claim to it.

After much contemplation, Diga said, "So why should we alone take the blame? Why should only Shabars get trapped in a false case? I'm going to tell the others. After all, they too revere the arjun. What do you say?"

Who knows how long the arjun had stood at that intersection. No one had really noticed it all these years. It was as if the tree had been there from time immemorial and would be there for time eternal. But now, all of a sudden it had become enormously important for everyone. As if it was a symbol of their existence!

The Forest Department did not control only the jungles, but the fallow land too. So where could the Shabars go? They had simply begun to wander from place to place. Wherever they saw a green patch of jungle land, they would settle down. Then the jungles would start disappearing. The fallow land would be sold off. Once again the Shabars would be homeless.

When the arjun had been a young tree, the Shabars had offered prayers to it before going on hunting expeditions. Now that it was mature, how grand it was! A shiny bark, the top touching the sky. On full-moon nights, the tree and moonlight seemed like one. During Chaitra and Baishakh, its spread of leaves provided such shade. It meant so much to them. That arjun at the crossing ...

Pitambar asked, "For how long has the arjun been guarding us? That one tree is the entire jungle for us. And our few families, the children of the forest. Now Mahato wants that very tree?"

"What can we do? Everything belongs to Bishal babu and Ram babu."

"Till we had built our huts, we lived under the arjun. Only later did Mahato give us the land to build our huts ..." went on Pitambar.

Diga put in his bit, "Didn't the Santhals come to it for shelter and consolation after Haldar had burnt their shanties?"

One by one they began to recall stories about the arjun tree. Each one realized that their lives and fate were inextricably linked with that of the arjun. Society and the system had continually persecuted, exploited and almost obliterated this handful of tribals from the face of the earth. Now the same fate awaited the arjun tree, the last mute symbol of their existence.

"Bishal babu is going to town. We must collect the cash from him before he leaves," said Diga.

"You will cut the tree then?"

"Five people should be enough to do the job. We'll ask for one hundred rupees, what do you say?"

Frequent visits to the jail and constant exploitation by society had taught the Shabars to mask their true feelings and intentions. One face was presented to the Mahatos of the world, while the other one remained hidden. In the days of the British, the Shabars were the only ones who could be relied upon to set police stations and check posts on fire. Today the babus were dependent on them, for these same Shabars performed the all-important tasks of land encroachment, crop theft, disposal of corpses and clearing government owned forests.

So who would be so dumb as to go to jail for cutting one single tree?

Diga gave a shrewd, cunning laugh. "You don't worry about it," he told the others. After all, he knew the alphabet, had been to the jails of districts as far apart as Jamshedpur, Chaibasa, Medinipur and Bankura.

Bishal babu was assured that by the time he returned from the town, the job would be done. "Go and conduct your election meetings with an easy mind. Give us the money. When you come back, you'll see that the tree is not there."

"Make sure that Ram babu doesn't get a hint of what is happening."

"Why, isn't he giving you the truck?"

"Yes, but he'll still create a big fuss. Also, take care that no one outside the district gets news of it."

"We'll see, babu."

On the surface, politicians hoisted different flags, but underneath, they were like sugar in milk. No conflict of interest when it came down to brass tacks.

Bishal babu, you have taught the foolish Shabars many a lesson, haven't you – what they call non-formal education!

The leaders of the two opposite camps abuse each other in public meetings. The cadre members do not understand all this. Abuses, petty quarrels and occasional bloodshed are all part of the political system. There is bound to be some dispute over the arjun too. But then, how many people would really support Ram Haldar? The entire village was under Bishal Mahato's sway.

A trip to the town really becomes frenzied, thought Bishal Mahato. On the way there are speeches and gatherings at the public halls and bazaars to be attended to. In the town, so many chores have to be taken care of. Get the moped light repaired, buy a new lantern, a shawl for the wife, some medicines ...

Satisfied with his trip, Bishal Mahato was returning to Bandihi. The problem of votes had been taken care of. Oh god! When would they build a proper road to the village? Nengshai, Tetka, stream after stream, and then the descent down the bamboo bridge. After that, the tortuous way through slippery paths and uneven roads.

But as he neared the village, his head reeled.

Against the backdrop of the deep blue sky, the majestic arjun tree stood with its head held high – like a guardian of the village, keeping vigil from its lofty post. Once upon a time, this land used to be guarded by hundreds of leafy sentinels. One by one, they have all gone, leaving no trace. Only the arjun is left now. Alone, to guard this devastated, neglected, humiliated land of his.

Unbidden, a proverb flashed through Bishal Mahato's mind, "The leaves of the arjun tree are like the tongue of man."

All around boomed the sound of the dhol-dhamsa-damak and the strains of the nagra. An agitated Bishal Mahato rushed into the village. A huge crowd had gathered around the arjun. Its trunk was covered with aakondo garlands.

Haldar was standing at the perimeter of the crowd, holding on to his bicycle.

"What happened?" asked Mahato.

"The gram-devata has made them do it," answered Haldar.

"What? Which ill-begotten fellow says so?"

"Diga had a dream, it seems. You paid him money in the dream and instructed him to build a concrete base around the trunk. People from all the tribes – Santhal, Khedia, Shohish, Bhumij – have now gathered to make their offerings."

"To the gram-devata?"

"Yes, and the crowds have not stopped coming. There is practically a mela on. We'd thought these fellows were fools. But they have made fools of us, Mahato!"

Bishal stepped forward to taste the full flavour of his defeat.

What a stupendous crowd! Ketu was dancing away like a maniac, going round and round with his dholok.

Bishal was suddenly afraid. This tree, these people – he knew them all. He knew them very well. And yet, today they seemed like strangers.

Fear. An uncomprehending fear gripped him.

"Arjun" was first published in Bangla in the *Dainik Bartaman*, 1984. This translation was first published by Katha in *Wordsmiths* in March 1996.

The FISHMONGER
BOLWAR MAHAMAD KUNHI

translated from Kannada by H Y Sharada Prasad

One could have sworn by any god that the young man in his twenties, who stood on the threshold seeking permission to enter, the man with wide eyes and a pleasant smile, did not have an iota of faith in astrology. If Adram Byari had not dropped in the previous evening at dusk and explained everything, Subraya Jois would have been more startled than puzzled by the visit of this man who had never before come to his house.

Jois gestured to the young man and bade him enter. He did so and sat opposite Jois on a straw mat with his feet tucked under him, like a man at namaaz. The radiance of youth was enhanced by the attar, Jannatul Firdaus, that he had sprinkled on himself.

Jois took some cowrie shells in his hand and cast them on the floor. He pulled a few of them together, brushing the rest to one side. He bent his fingers and then opened them, one by one, obviously making some calculations. Then he shut his eyes in the manner of a man looking for the answer to a riddle. A moment or two later, he opened his eyes and, with the triumphant smile of a man who knew it all, asked the young visitor in a playful voice, "Isn't your name Razzak?"

"Yes."

"Weren't you watching a film at this hour last Friday?"

"Yes."

"And you didn't go to the theatre today because you wanted to be here?"

"Yes."

"And also, before coming here, you didn't go to the Liberty Hotel, as you do every Friday, but went instead to an Udipi eating place for a vegetarian meal?"

"Yes."

"And you are planning to buy a second-hand car and you are here because you want to consult me?"

"Yes."

"Now tell me, how did I come to know all this?"

"Because Adram Byari of the cloth shop told you."

They both burst into laughter. There was no trace of reserve now. Razzak shyly placed before Jois a ten rupee note he had hidden in his fist.

"Adram Byari hadn't told me about this money. Or did he give you a special coaching?"

Razzak caught the disapproval in Jois's tone and did not attempt an answer.

Subraya Jois's reputation as an astrologer was well-known from Sakleshpur above the ghats to Kasargod on the coast. It was a matter of record that marriages made on the basis of the horoscopes he had studied and matched had endured without exception. When war had broken out for the second time between Pakistan and India, he had forecast, in the very first week, that India would score a swift victory, and the prediction had been widely reported in the newspapers. This wiry man with a bent nose, large ears and shining eyes, this man who was on the threshold of sixty and commanded instant respect from anyone who saw him ... such a person's

The Fishmonger

disapproval was something Razzak did not know how to deal with. He wondered whether he had done the right thing at all in coming to Jois at Adram Byari's bidding.

It did not take Jois much effort to read what was going on in the young man's mind. His face revealed it all. Jois craned his neck towards the door at the back of the room and said aloud, "Oh lady of the house, look, your Fish Clock is here in person."

Jois's wife knew someone had come in and had been waiting behind the door for the summons. Even so, she was taken aback to see Razzak.

The young man who sat like a disciple on the mat was no stranger. She saw him every afternoon, barring the three or four months of the rainy season. A couple of minutes after four, his bicycle carrying baskets of fish passed in front of the house, Razzak would announce his progress by pressing the rubber horn attached to the handlebar.

From Jois's house one could see the knot of women and children waiting for the bicycle at the end of the street.

That was the terminus of Razzak's daily journey. By the time he arrived there, he would have sold the contents of the two baskets tied to the carrier of the bicycle and he would be left with the fish in the two palm leaf bags that hung from the handlebar. It was not his habit to haggle and it did not take him much time to dispose of his stock. After that he went to the public pond at the end of Post Office Road for a bath.

It was not only Razzak's customers who knew the various stops on his daily route. The smell of his fish assailed the nostrils of everyone on his beat, whether they were fish eaters or not. His punctuality had earned him the nickname "Radio Time Razzak." And Jois called him the Fish Clock.

Jois had publicly paid him a tribute a couple of years ago. This is how it had happened: Jois was giving a discourse on values in life and the meaning of devotion at the Ganesha festival in the main temple of the town. He had expatiated on the idea that devotion consisted, not in shutting one's eyes and singing hymns, but in doing one's work with utmost dedication and without any expectation of reward. "Let me give you an example," Jois had gone on to say. "Take Razzak, the youngster who sells fish. There is no difference between bhakti and the thoroughness with which he goes about his work." These words of Jois had become the talk of the town.

To recognize Razzak, you needed eyes only on one day of the week. On other days the nose would do. On Fridays, Razzak took a break from his work. From ten thirty to twelve thirty he was at the government pond on Post Office Road, giving himself a good scrub from head to toe. Why, even the white rubber sandals he wore were cleaned with the bath soap he used. Then at the stroke of one, he was at the mosque. His clothes could serve as an illustration of the phrase "shining bright like lightning": A milk-white dhoti, a sparkling white full-sleeved shirt, and a white handkerchief with a green or blue border tucked around the nape of his neck to protect the collar of his shirt, and the perfume. His presence on Fridays was announced by the perfume he used so liberally.

After namaaz he took a rickshaw and rode to the Liberty Military Hotel (it was called "military" because

The Fishmonger

it served meat). From there, again by rickshaw, he made his way to the Apsara cinema hall, where a new film was released every Friday. The left corner seat in the front row of the balcony was reserved for him by the management. After the matinee show Razzak sat on the jagali of Adram Byari's cloth shop until sunset, hardly talking to anyone. At eight, he rose and went back to the same eating place where he had his afternoon meal. And by nine, he was back home.

After the death of Razzak's mother, there had not been a single day when Jois's wife had not thought of sending for him to enquire after his welfare. She and Razzak's mother had been born in the same town and had come to Muthuppadi as brides around the same time. Whenever there was a feast in Jois's house, a packet of eatables was set apart for Razzak's mother. Razzak had never accompanied his mother, except perhaps as a child, when she may have brought him, perched on her waist.

This was the first time Jois's wife was seeing him from this near and so surprised was she that she didn't know what to say.

Jois turned towards his wife and said in a teasing voice, "Tell me, have any of your sons ever been so spotlessly clean?"

She retorted, "The smell of fish suits him better than all that perfume he has poured on himself."

"Let her be," Jois said to Razzak. "She has no patience with anyone who is neat and clean. She wants the whole world to be full of good-for-nothings like her two sons."

Razzak did not know what to make of this banter

between a woman who had never spoken to him before and a man who was the town's most respected person.

Razzak had been too young when his father died to have any memories of him. His mother had died within a year of his becoming a fishmonger. He had no one in the world to call his own, no one who bothered whether he was alive or dead, except perhaps Adram Byari. With all the others, his dealings were limited to the buying and selling of fish.

The daily fish trade in Muthuppadi was around six or seven thousand rupees. The supply came from Mangalore, forty miles away. A lorry arrived around noon every day, proclaiming its arrival with a very distinctive toot. This was the signal for the marketplace to come alive. On days when the catch was plentiful, a couple of cars followed the lorry. As soon as the horn was heard, fish sellers got busy. They tucked up their lungis and came, pushing their bicycles as close to the lorry as possible. When the baskets were being unloaded from the lorry, urchins would dart to and fro to snatch any fish that slipped to the ground, out-manoeuvring the dogs which were there with the same intent. Razzak had mastered his trade as one of these light-footed boys who sold the fish they managed to lay their hands on. Now he was an established fishmonger. And in a week he would have a car of his own.

"So, are you going to just stand there, staring at him or can you offer him at least a tumbler of milk?" Jois asked his wife. When she went inside, Jois turned to Razzak and said to him in a serious tone, "Listen to me, young man. When Adram Byari came to me yesterday, I told him that only a man who did not know

The Fishmonger

his mind worried about the future. You are not such a one. You are clear in your mind about what you want to do. I hear you have even paid an advance for the car. Suppose I consulted the cowrie shells and told you that the deal would not be profitable, would that stop you from buying the car?"

Razzak did not know what to say. The deal had been struck. An advance of two thousand rupees had been paid. All that remained now was to sign seven or eight documents at the office of Naik Finance the following Monday and the car would become his. It would not be very difficult to pay the monthly instalment of seven hundred rupees. There was no question of his going back on the transaction.

A smile played on Jois's face when he found Razzak at a loss for words. He got up, and so did Razzak. Just then Jois's wife came into the room with a tumbler of milk. Jois took it from her hand and, cupping it in both palms, offered it to Razzak, "Drink it before you go. May good fortune always be with you," he said.

Razzak took the tumbler in all solemnity, sat down on the floor and drank the milk. Jois's wife, who was watching this scene, broke the silence. She bent down and picked up the ten rupee note which Razzak had placed at the edge of the mat, saying, "This money is mine, we have earned it." It was Jois's turn to be dumbfounded.

If Subraya Jois should say that the sun would not rise the next day, there was one man who would defend him with all conviction. That was Narayana Prabhu. His faith in Jois's predictions was total.

Prabhu was not only the sub-postmaster of the town of Muthuppadi but also one of the pillars of its society. It was he who had organized the very first Ganesha festival in the Sahasra Lingeshwara Temple with much fanfare. And it was he who had persuaded Jois to give a discourse on the nature of dharma during the festival.

Normally Prabhu would not presume to question even one word that issued from Jois. But he was also a great believer in certain proprieties. He wondered whether it was proper for Jois to drag in the name of a Muslim fish seller to illustrate the idea of dharma. With his vast knowledge of the Vedas, the Shastras and the Puranas, Jois could have come up with more suitable examples from our own tradition, if only he had given it a moment's thought. Could he not have spoken of Dharmaraja, of Hanuman, of Sabari? But he chose to mention Razzak, of all the people. What had come over him?

Not that Prabhu questioned the validity of what Jois had said about Razzak and his thoroughness. Why, Prabhu himself waited for the horn of Razzak's bicycle every afternoon to call out to his wife that it was time to make tea.

There was another reason why Prabhu was flustered. Ananta Bhatta was the most contrary man in town. No matter what was being discussed, he would start his argument with "It's not like that, swamy, but like this ..." As a consequence he had earned the nickname No-But Bhatt. Even he had agreed with Jois on this matter. "I just can't believe that this boy was born to a Moplah. What courtesy! What scrupulousness! If by any chance Razzak sees me on the road, he gets off his bicycle at once, moves to the edge of the road, and waits until I pass. If we ignored the fact that he goes to a mosque once a week, tell me in what respect is he inferior to us?" Bhatta had asked.

All this had happened two years ago and it came as a flashback to Prabhu one afternoon.

He was locking up the post office for the day when Adram Byari rushed panting up to him, saying, "I have to make an urgent call. I hear our Razzak has met with an accident."

The call went through to the Mangalore Hospital quickly enough. They learnt that Razzak's car had been hit by a lorry and had fallen into a ditch at a bend on the Bantwal road. Fortunately Razzak had not been seriously hurt. The car, however, was a wreck.

After Adram Byari left, Prabhu sat down on the doorstep, too dazed even to lock his office. Barely three months since Razzak had bought his car, and already an accident? Prabhu found it hard to believe that Subraya Jois had not known this would happen. If he had known it, why had he not warned Razzak, Razzak for whom he had such regard?

Adram Byari had told him all about how Razzak had gone to Jois for advice, how Jois, with not so much as a glance at the cowries, had sent off Razzak with the strange words. You do not need your future to be read. Prabhu had not attached much importance to it then. But, in retrospect, Jois's behaviour appeared inexplicable and out of character. What could be at the root of Jois's ambivalence? It was all a riddle to Prabhu.

He decided to go to Jois's house, carrying this bundle of doubts in his head. Even as he went up the steps he called out, "Have you heard, Jois-re? Our Radio

Time, our Razzak, met with an accident this afternoon. The car is all smashed up."

Jois was just about to place a lighted agarbathi in front of the framed picture of God. "What did you say?" he exclaimed and sat down heavily, as if his legs had given way beneath him.

Prabhu was alarmed. He sat next to Jois and to make amends for the panic he had created, added, "But, there's no need to worry, Jois-re. Adram Byari phoned Mangalore from my office. The boy's luck is as solid as a grindstone. He escaped with just a few scratches. They said he should be out of hospital in a day or two. If anyone else had been in such an accident, it would have been difficult to recover a single bone. Adram Byari thinks the car will have to be sold off as scrap."

Jois sat motionless. He did not even look at Prabhu.

Prabhu was quiet for a few minutes. But he could not stop himself from asking, though with great hesitation, "I am told that those people do not believe in our astrology and things like that. But is it true that you sent him away when he came to see you?"

Jois sat unstirring like the trunk of a tree.

Prabhu moved closer to Jois and said, in a whisper, "Did you know all this would happen? Is that why you did not go through with consulting the cowries?"

Jois flinched as if he had been lashed with a whip. He stole a quick glance at Prabhu and was reassured to find a sarcasm on his countenance. "Oh my God," he murmured, covering his ears with his palms. Prabhu had known Jois for more than twenty years. Not once had he doubted Jois's integrity. What had driven him now to ask this question? "There must have been some error in my calculations. I must re-check," said Jois after a few moments and dragged himself back into his house.

Adram Byari was ready to stand before any dargah built for the glory of Allah the Merciful, and swear that if Subraya Jois had had any inkling whatsoever that Razzak's car would be smashed up within three months, he would have said so in so many words that afternoon Razzak had gone to him. So when Narayana Prabhu went to Adram Byari's house with Ananta Bhatta to tell him that Jois had not touched his cowries for more than a month now, he did not know what to make of the news.

Narayana Prabhu had heard rumours a week ago that Jois was no longer practising astrology because he was unwell. He had not made much of it. After all, when a man is on the wrong side of sixty, to be in poor health is not surprising. But now that a month had passed and people were talking about Jois refusing to even look at the cowries, Prabhu was deeply distressed. He was not the sort to share his inner thoughts with anyone else. But he had no doubt that Jois's practice had come to an abrupt end the day that he, Prabhu, had gone to him with the news of Razzak's accident. If anyone found that out, Prabhu would find it impossible to live in that town. He wondered if he should not go to Jois, fall at his feet and ask for forgiveness. If Jois forgave him, well and good. But if he didn't, it would be like giving a stick to a man and asking to be thrashed. It would be humiliating. The thought of the injustice he might have done to Jois tormented Prabhu day and night, robbing him of even his sleep.

Meanwhile Razzak had returned home after spending four or five days in hospital. He had dropped in to see Prabhu a couple of times to tell him of his troubles with the insurance people and with Naik Finance. These visits only deepened Prabhu's feeling of guilt. Once he almost asked, Have you met Jois, but managed to change the question at the last minute to "Have the insurance people promised to compensate you?"

"Partly. I think it might be more sensible to hand over the car to them than get it repaired. Luckily nothing happened to my hands and legs. I can get back to my business and one day perhaps buy a better car, maybe even two," Razzak replied, leaving Prabhu even more perturbed.

It was one of the longest months in Prabhu's life. He found it more and more difficult to bear the agony all by himself. Finally, he decided to take Ananta Bhatta into confidence.

No-But Bhatt heard him out patiently. Then he said, typically, "It's not like that, Prabhu-re. Let me tell you, the stars are the same whether one is a Hindu, a Muslim, or a Christian. Haven't the newspapers written about Americans consulting our astrologers before launching their rockets? If you think Jois deliberately chose not to consult his shells, that would amount to saying he knew what was in store for Razzak. There must be no connection, as you choose to think, between the accident and his giving up astrology."

None of No-But Bhatt's arguments made any sense to Prabhu. It was like holding a lamp behind one to light one's way ahead.

"Look here, Bhatta-re," said Prabhu. "It's true I came to you and told you everything, but it was not so you could tell me what is right and what is wrong, but to see if you had any suggestions as to how I can go to Jois and apologize to him. Tomorrow is a Sunday. You must go with me to Jois's house. But there's one important point you must remember. Whatever I have told you today must remain between the two of us. If anyone ever gets to know about it, I will have recourse to one thing only – a rope."

Prabhu's tone showed he had come to a decision. To put him at ease, Bhatt said, "What do I lose by going with you? And what do I gain by broadcasting our discussion? I shall be at your house at lunchtime. We'll go after lunch. Elephants are not going to turn into horses in the meanwhile, are they?"

He was as good as his word, arriving at Prabhu's house at lunchtime. Consumed as he was by the confusion in his mind, Prabhu could barely force a couple of mouthfuls down his throat. But Bhatta enjoyed his meal, even asking for second helpings.

He finished his meal with a satisfied burp.

Just as Bhatta stood up, saying, "Shall we leave?" Prabhu suggested, "Won't it be better if we took our friend Adram Byari of the cloth shop along? After all it was Byari who sent Razzak to Jois. If he exculpates Jois of responsibility, that would make Jois feel better."

Ananta Bhatta, the "but" and "however" man, agreed at once. He was ready for anything that would lessen Prabhu's worry.

The two made their way to Byari's cloth shop.

Byari ordered two cups of tea for them from the adjoining Ganesh Vilas. After hearing Prabhu out, Byari said, "If Allah draws a line and says it shall be this, nobody can alter that line even a little bit. Take it from me. The man who has lost his car has kept a cool head. Why are you behaving as if the sky has fallen on you?"

And he went on to say, "But I agree we – all three of us – should meet Jois. Today is as good a day as any."

"No matter what god I swear by, my husband refuses to listen to me, Prabhu-re." Jois's wife said to them. "Now that you are all here, please try and persuade him," she said, giving the three guests some jaggery and water to quench their thirst. She sat down on the floor leaning against the jamb of the inner door.

There was no sign of Jois.

"Is he resting?" asked Adram Byari.

Ananta Bhatta cut in, "It is this way, Akka. In this world most people think only of themselves. Our Jois is not like that. He is like the mother who always thinks of her children. There is a reason behind everything he does. As Lord Krishna said in the Bhagvad Gita ..."

"Whatever Lord Krishna might say, my lord and master says his horse has only three legs," Jois's wife said, matter-of-factly.

"Will you go in and tell him we are here?"

Jois's wife looked at the clock on the wall and replied, "There is no need for anyone to call him. When the clock strikes four, out he will come like a clockwork doll that has been wound up. Wait for just two more minutes and you will see for yourselves."

The three exchanged glances, not able to make out what Jois's wife meant.

A silence fell on the group. They sat there, gazing at the old clock, waiting for the minute hand to touch twelve. The tension broke when it chimed four times.

Jois's wife did not stir.

They saw the curtain of the inner door being pushed aside, and Jois's shrunken frame came into view. The three visitors who had been sitting on a bench in the front room, stood up.

Jois smiled vaguely at them without seeming to have really noticed them. Prabhu brought his hands together in a namaskara; Jois did not return the greeting. Instead, like a sleepwalker, he turned and walked towards the front door, crossed the threshold and went down the steps to sit on the last step. His eyes were rivetted on the road.

Ananta Bhatta rose, made a signal to Adram Byari with his eye, and followed Jois.

"No one, not even God can get a word out of him when he sits there," Jois's wife said, in a choked voice, beating her forehead with her palm. "He has had just one refrain since last month. Whatever I say, he silences me by putting a finger to his lips and saying, The fisherboy *will* come again. What can I say to his obsession?"

Suddenly, Adram Byari exclaimed loudly, "Yah Allah!"

The three others looked at him in alarm.

Adram Byari said in a ringing voice, "Jois is one hundred per cent right! Razzak is starting his business again. And look, he's starting today!"

Even before Adram Byari could complete his words, and as if to prove Jois's prediction, Razzak rode by, blowing the horn on his bicycle.

"The Fishmonger" was first published in Kannada as "Meenu Maruvavanu" in *Prajavani*, Deepavali Special Issue, October 1993, Bangalore.

The WILL
AHMAD YUSUF

translated from Urdu by Nadeem Ahmed

Just before he breathed his last, the old man summoned his sons and spelt out his will. "Children, after I am gone, all that I have shall be yours. Share it among yourselves, but make sure that none of you gets more or less than the others. And do not quarrel with each other."

Then he departed from this world.

The sons were grief stricken. For the first time they felt as if the roof above their heads had been blown off in a terrible storm, and they were left to fend for themselves. The prospect of leading their lives without the comforting presence of their father slowly dawned upon them and they groped along in the unfamiliar world. While their father was alive, they had not a care, for the old man had taken complete charge of their lives, and they had looked to him for their smallest needs.

There were six of them. The youngest one, Fahim, was to take his High School exam that year. Aleem, was his elder and in the final year of intermediate. Wasim, the next in line, had struggled his way through graduation, and believed that he had had enough of studies. He got himself registered at the Employment Exchange, and dashed off applications for any job he happened to hear about. After Wasim came Azeem, in the first year of MA. His subject was History, but he could never truly understand it. Dates and events confused him, and he would get historical events all mixed up. Older than him was Saleem who had finished his graduation while his father was alive. He had a job as a science teacher in a school. Saleem was at peace with himself and the world. A firm believer in fate, he was convinced that the job of a school teacher was pre-ordained for him. He also had a family – two small kids and a devoted wife, who had learnt to be happy with whatever her husband provided, for she knew that no amount of prodding would change Saleem's attitude to life.

In a lighter moment, Saleem would often hum a favourite tune, *"Ek bangla baney nyaara ..."* Although the song was meant to please his wife, it only got her piqued. She believed that daydreaming was the preserve of the weak and Saleem lacked the determination to turn his dreams into reality. Besides, a man who had surrendered his life to Fate had no business to have such ambitions.

Nadeem, who was the eldest of the brothers, was a good seven years older than Saleem. This gap between the old man's children would have been much narrower had his two daughters and a son survived beyond infancy. By the time the old man retired after crossing the age of seventy two, Nadeem had gradually been entrusted with the reins of business and property. Nadeem had three sons. The eldest one, who was in High School, was as old as his youngest uncle, Fahim. The other two were studying in the eighth and sixth standards respectively.

Strangely enough, when Nadeem found himself at the helm of affairs, he started seeing visions of kings

~ THE WILL ~

and princes. He perceived himself the heir apparent since he was the eldest of the princes and had the right to wear the crown after the king died. And once he was crowned, he saw himself sentencing his brothers to death just as earlier kings had done, in order to keep his throne safe. Or he could appoint them governors of distant provinces, thus removing them permanently from the palace. He found the latter option appealing for, after all, he was a kind and generous man and could not take the lives of his brothers. So he decided to send them off to rule over their respective provinces, in this case, different portions of the house in which they lived.

But one condition in his father's will played havoc with his flights of fancy – No one ought to get more or less than the other. The rest of the will was fine, but how could he conform to this stipulation? He worried about it for a few days, but very soon consolidated his position. He began to consider himself a worthy successor to the throne vacated by his father, and his brothers, weak and powerless provincial governors under a strong and powerful central authority.

The brothers were allotted separate quarters within the house. Saleem was married and had a family, so he was given a large bedroom alongside a small living room, a veranda and a toilet.

The room adjoining Saleem's was occupied by the history scholar. He was also permitted to use Saleem's bathroom. These rooms opened out on to a small courtyard, across which were three more rooms, each occupied by the other three brothers.

A maid had been employed to cook for them, but Nadeem and Saleem's wives also lent a hand for a couple of hours in the mornings and at tea time. The kitchen was a place for chatting, laughter and good humoured banter. Food was sent up to each room, and was the kind one would associate with a jail or a hospital. Every meal invariably consisted of potatoes or any vegetable that was cheap because it was at the peak of its season. The dal was watery and no amount of stirring would bring up a solid particle. It was accompanied by cold chapatis or equally cold rice. This fare was grandiosely referred to as "Estate Meals."

Besides their college fees, the brothers were allowed a meagre allowance of Rs 25 per month. The youngest, Fahim, and his elder, Aleem, had formed a partnership and did many things together. They pooled in their pocket money, and took turns to handle the monthly expenses. They ate their meals together and often made efforts to enliven the insipid fare with kebabs or an occasional omelette cooked in Saleem's kitchen. They sometimes indulged their sweet tooth with a small piece of gud or with gajak from the bazaar.

Apart from the Estate Kitchen, Nadeem and Saleem each had a kerosene stove in a corner of their respective rooms, referred to as their mini kitchen. The stoves were lit in a furtive manner and food was cooked behind a veil of secrecy. While the activities of the mini kitchens were kept hidden from the four brothers, Nadeem and Saleem kept them from each other too. Or so they thought. For the aroma of these secretly cooked meals betrayed them. Then there were Nadeem's sons, Shamshad, Dilshad and Naushad – they often dropped in at Saleem's quarters and talked about food which was not cooked in the Estate Kitchen as they caught fragrant whiffs emanating from their uncle's mini kitchen!

Wasim had by then finished his graduation and was looking for a job. He took up a tuition or two in order to augment his income. The tuitions fetched him a valuable Rs 100 or Rs 150 which, along with his monthly allowance, made up a decent sum. Much of it was spent in the process of job hunting. There was stationery to be bought and applications posted. Most employers insisted on postal orders too. Out of the remaining amount he would buy the fruit of the season and share it with his two younger brothers and Azeem. His sole concern was to find himself a good job and stand on his own feet. To be independent and a master of his own life was indeed an obsession with him. However, he was not sure what he wanted to do. One day he aired his views in the presence of his brothers. Azeem immediately asked him what he meant by standing on his own feet. "To be able to meet my day-to-day needs," he replied. The two looked at him in consternation. "Will you give up the Estate Meals then?" asked Azeem, incredulously.

"No, my own home ..." fumbled Wasim.

"Do you mean to say that you will move out of the Estate?" they asked in unison, alarmed at their brother's talk of turning renegade. Wasim had to beat a hasty retreat at their unexpected onslaught.

Azeem then said, very sternly, "Have you lost your mind? Have you already forgotten Abbu's last words, After I am gone, everything shall be yours?" With a deliberate pause, he added, "You will leave all this and go away?" That was the last time Wasim had talked about becoming independent. Instead, he gave vent to his stifled ambitions by turning philosophical whenever the topic came up. He would say, "If a man does not have the urge to earn a living, he would be no different from a beast."

Azeem graduated with good marks. Since he had good grades at High School too, he got a part-time job with a coaching institute which trained boys for High School, Intermediate and BA exams. The job earned him Rs 250 a month. Along with his pocket money, this was enough to buy good clothes – his only obsession.

Every Id, the boys were presented two sets of clothes for daily wear, one kurta pyjama set, two vests and a handkerchief, from the Estate. Since Azeem could afford other clothes besides the Estate largesse, he had some decent outfits to wear on special occasions. Wasim often borrowed Azeem's clothes when he went for his numerous interviews. Azeem was convinced that the graph of his career was steadily rising. The thought generated in him a good deal of optimism and kept him in high spirits.

After their father's demise, the four younger brothers gradually distanced themselves from their eldest brother Nadeem. They felt he belonged to another generation and was an outsider. But they could relate to Saleem, since the difference in their ages was not much.

Elder brother Nadeem and his wife had been considered the two pillars of the Estate even during their father's lifetime. But their authority was not absolute because their father had kept control of the business himself though he had handed over the household to the eldest daughter-in-law. Now that the old man was no more, they assumed complete command. On the day of Soyam, a ceremony held three days after a person's death, Nadeem sent for his brothers. He placed his hands on each of their heads, a gesture of blessing from a patriarch. Their eyes were moist, they had lumps in their throats. Then, Maulvi Irshad, who was always invited to family gatherings and special occasions, cleared his throat and said, "Your late father had wished to see you united and not quarrelling as everything in the Estate belongs to you all."

After spending a little time with the eldest brother, the younger ones returned to their rooms. Then Nadeem's wife went to each of them separately and wiped their tears. However, her efforts to console them only gave rise to a feeling of antipathy towards Nadeem and his wife. They felt that Nadeem was behaving like an elder family member showing sympathy for them on their bereavement, not as one who was equally affected by it. They realized that for him, nothing had changed. With such thoughts the closeness they had felt with their eldest brother, soon disappeared.

Six months had passed since their father's death and Nadeem was in full control of the family business. By now the younger brothers had started feeling uneasy about the affairs of the house and particularly about Nadeem's conduct and his role. They decided it was time they had a word with him about it. Saleem would go to him on their behalf and find out how he planned to divide their father's bequest. Saleem broached the subject cautiously.

"It has been six months since Abbu died. Don't you think it is time that we went ahead with the division of the property?"

Nadeem replied gravely, "If each of us takes his

share and goes his own way, imagine how troubled Abbu's soul would be. After all, he did say that everything belonged to us!"

Saleem accepted the bait of Nadeem's argument and conceded that such an act would indeed hurt their father's soul. However, there could be no harm in at least finding out what each one would get, even if they didn't actually divide the property. The issue rested there that day.

Actually, Saleem was too simple to get to the bottom of such matters. He was quite content with his school, his pupils, his wife and kids, and the two rooms they lived in. He had gone to Nadeem only because his wife and his younger brothers goaded him.

Now Nadeem and his wife knew how each of them felt.

A couple of days after the first anniversary of their father's death, Nadeem called his brothers to his room. When they got there, they found Maulvi Irshad with him. Nadeem began, "I saw Abbu in my dream last night." He paused to survey their faces and took one step forward. The others moved one step back. Then he continued, "As I said, I saw Abbu, dressed in a spotless white kurta pyjama, standing in a vast plain. He was warning us against a frightful storm which would be upon us any moment. He asked us to stand close together and fall flat on the ground upon his signal in order to save ourselves from the storm. We then saw a huge army coming at us in a cloud of dust, like waves in an ocean. The army consisted of a large number of foot soldiers, cavalry and elephants."

Then Maulvi Irshad expounded the meaning of the

dream. "May Allah's mercy be upon us! Your venerable father wishes to see you united, so that you can weather all storms in your lives."

The brothers heard him out, then returned to their respective quarters.

Azeem had finished his MA and was now running around for his PhD. Wasim had succeeded in getting a job with the Irrigation Department. Aleem had finished Intermediate and was now studying for his BA, while Fahim had passed his matriculation and moved into Intermediate.

One day, while the brothers were sitting together at Saleem's place, Fahim suggested that it was about time Azeem got married. Saleem agreed. "Yes, he ought to. Really, he ought to."

Azeem, a trifle annoyed, replied, "Despite your insistence I am not going to marry yet."

"Why?" everyone asked in unison.

"You ask me why? Just think, what do I have to offer my wife except tasteless Estate Meals? Saleem bhaiya has a job, and he can afford to give his family something better than that. I am still without any means of livelihood. What shall I tell my wife? That I have nothing of my own, yet everything is mine?"

Azeem's outburst disconcerted them all, for it was the truth. They also noticed that Nadeem's eldest son, who was sitting amidst them, had quietly left.

A few days later, Nadeem sent for them. Once again they found Maulvi Irshad with him. They got ready to listen to another one of Nadeem's dreams.

"I had a strange dream last night," he said. "I saw that we were standing on the banks of a river. Suddenly

Abbu appeared from somewhere. He took a small stone from his pocket and threw it flat over the water. The stone skipped on the surface six times, producing a ripple each time. Thus there were six ripples in all, each merging into the other, then getting obliterated from the surface."

Maulvi Irshad promptly proceeded to interpret the dream. "Allah be praised, what a significant dream. Your great father was trying to tell you that like the ripples on the surface of the water, which rise separately, you too have your individual identities. But just as they merge and become one in the end, your independent personalities should merge into a single whole – the Family."

One day Nadeem's wife went over to Saleem's room and asked Azeem to come there too. She told him, "Your brother was talking about advocate Ahmed Ali Sahib's daughter. He has her in mind for you. What do you think?"

Azeem instantly retorted, "Badi bhabhi, it was different during your days. These are different times. What would I say if the girl asked me what I did for a living? Simply telling her that I have everything won't satisfy her."

Badi bhabhi was infuriated by Azeem's candid reply. She couldn't remain there a moment longer. Saleem rebuked his younger brother mildly, "Was it really necessary to hurt Bhabhi's feelings?"

Azeem replied, "Forgive me, Bhaiya, but I am not a sufi like you." And the matter rested there.

By now Azeem had registered for a PhD. He had also resigned from his part-time job. Wasim had started giving him Rs 100 a month for his expenses, and Rs 50 to each of the two younger brothers. He kept a small amount for himself and the rest he stashed away in his Post Office Savings Account.

Three years had elapsed since their father's death. Once again, Nadeem called his brothers over to his quarters. Maulvi Irshad was in customary attendance, indicating to them that another account of their brother's dream was on the way.

Nadeem began, "I saw Abbu in my dream last night. He was standing with us under a high wall, which was in a dilapidated condition. He kept looking at the wall, then said, This wall needs your special attention."

Maulvi Irshad was quick with his customary elucidation of the dream. "Allah be praised, your father was a man of great vision. He wanted the high wall of your family to remain standing. And you must maintain it regularly, keep it in good condition."

The five brothers listened to him in silence, their heads bowed. Then they quietly returned to their rooms. When they met again the same evening, Fahim said aloud, "I really don't understand the truth of Nadeem bhaiya's dreams!"

Before anyone else could express an opinion, Saleem said, "One cannot question the validity of dreams because dreams are mentioned in the Sura Yusuf of the Holy Koran too." After that the conversation turned away from the subject which Fahim had sought to raise.

It was Aleem's final year of BA and he was studying really hard. He would often say that he had to work towards securing a career and not see visions. His brothers reminded him that there was nothing wrong in imagining happier days. Their minds turned once again to their father's will. Once again the five of them conferred about the division of property and whatever else their father had left them. They decided that they should talk to their eldest brother about it. So they went to him and brought up the subject. Nadeem listened to them patiently and said, "You are absolutely correct. I am also of the same view as you. But whenever I think of taking a positive step towards that end, Abbu appears in my dream and tells me in so many ways that he will not approve of any division of the property. Let me consult a lawyer. Saleem, will you come with me?"

They were still working out the manner of dividing the property, when, one morning, they were summoned to Nadeem's quarters just before they left for office. Maulvi Irshad, a permanent fixture on such occasions, was there too. As was the practice, the eldest brother took one step forward, the younger five went one step back. Nadeem began his narration, "Dear brothers, I had a dream last night in which Abbu, wearing his tehmad, was sitting on the bed. We brothers were standing around him. Abbu had a bagful of coins in his hands which he was tossing up and catching. His face exuded happiness and satisfaction. He was saying, Children, this is all yours. All yours."

Maulvi Irshad ran his fingers through his beard and came out with another one of his explanations. "What a fantastic dream, what a fair-minded father you had. He was telling you that the wealth of the family and you brothers should stay together just like the coins in the bag."

That evening the five met to discuss the ongoing dreams. Wasim asked Saleem, "Do you think Abbu really doesn't want us to get our share? What is the truth of these dreams, I want to know!"

"Not the truth of the dreams, but of their interpretation," Saleem explained.

Azeem had spent two years finishing his PhD, Aleem had completed his graduation and had taken admission in MA in English, and Fahim was in the first year of BA. All three of them began to hope for better times ahead.

"What shall I do after my PhD?" Azeem would ask.

"To start with, you can add 'Dr' to your name," Saleem's wife would say jokingly. But it hardly ever amused him.

"Will I have to run from pillar to post for a job just like Wasim had to?"

In one voice the others would reassure him, "Oh no. Insha Allah you will certainly get a lecturer's post, even though there are not so many government jobs."

Aleem too worried about his career. MA, PhD, then what?

This time when the summons came from Nadeem, they were about to leave for their offices and colleges.

Wasim asked Saleem, "Bhaiya, is it really necessary for all of us to go and listen to yet another dream and its explanation?"

Saleem patted him lightly and said, "Come, let's see what he has to say this time."

Nadeem started, "Dear brothers, I saw Abbu in my dream last night. He was clad in his brocade sherwani, leading a baraat, his walking stick in hand." Nadeem interrupted his discourse to ask Saleem, "Saleem, you do remember Abbu's sherwani, don't you?"

"Yes, I do," Saleem nodded slowly.

"As I was saying, all of us were hardly a step behind him, but he insisted that we march together with him. There is great dignity in doing so, he said."

Maulvi Irshad came up with his explanation, "What a charming dream! Your great father was trying to tell you that you should always stay together. That is the key to happiness. Marriage denotes happiness and prosperity. What an interesting dream indeed!"

The brothers held a council that evening to take stock of the situation.

"It has been five years since Abbu died, and all we have got as our share is the taste of Nadeem bhaiya's obscure dreams," said Azeem.

"Hmm," muttered Wasim. They didn't know what more to say.

Azeem had applied in several places for the post of lecturer, but was also doing the rounds of government offices. Aleem was in the final year of MA, while Fahim had finished graduation and was wondering what to study next.

Once again the brothers were summoned by Nadeem. Once again they found Maulvi Irshad beside him. Both of them took one step forward and Nadeem began, "Brothers, I had a dream that we were going for a walk in a mango grove with our Abbu. Suddenly we spotted a qalmi mango tree laden with fruit. We all rushed towards it and tried to climb it when Abbu stopped us by raising his hand. He said, Only the eldest among you has the right to climb that tree. The others shall hold the sheet below it and collect the fruit Nadeem throws down ..."

~ The Will ~

Saleem, thoroughly fed up by now with Nadeem's dreams and Maulvi Irshad's opportunistic interpretations, raised a peremptory hand to silence him.

"We have heard enough about your dreams, and we can't take any more. You had the same relationship with Abbu as we had. Therefore last night he decided to appear in my dream," said Saleem. "We were enjoying a stroll in a beautiful garden and we saw an enormous potted plant. It had grown so large that its branches were touching the ground. Next to it were five empty pots. Abbu looked at them and said, This is not right. Ask the gardener to prune its branches and plant the cuttings in the five empty pots. This way, not only will the overgrown plant be shaped, there will be five more plants in the garden adding to its charm. It's surprising that you did not think of it earlier."

The five brothers gaped at Saleem with wide-eyed astonishment. They had not imagined that he too could employ the ruse of the dream so well. At this point, contrary to established practice, the five brothers took one step forward and came face to face with Nadeem. The eldest brother took one step back, his face contorted with rage and humiliation. Maulvi Irshad, of course, had disappeared from the scene.

The
DOOR
HIMANSHI SHELAT

translated from Gujarati by Darshana Dave

"You silly child, you're going to die like this one day. It's four days since, isn't your stomach paining? Can't you see everyone else goes there quite happily, only you, you are special, you shy, bashful girl!"

Savali forced herself to stand up as her mother blabbered on like this. But still, going across the khaadi gives her the shivers. Just two days ago thunder had rolled and rain lashed. Slippery slushy roads, dirty water gutters, one had to jump across them, all the way till the bushes in the distant groves. There too, across the soggy grass, completely flattened under who knows how many feet, to find one decent spot to squat is not easy. A frog jumps out, an earthworm wriggles on to your foot, you scream, your heart in your mouth, scared eyes darting around, you quickly finish what you have to do. Don't know how Savanti or Devu don't find anything wrong with it – wherever they like, they squat. No need to go so far trudging through the slush, who has the time to look at you, they say, giggling away. Everyone is doing their own business, who is going to look at whom? Absolutely shameless she is, this Savanti.

When it is still dark and not yet light in the early morning, many shadows are seen slinking along the zigzag paths in and around the creek. The whole scene appears very mysterious but really, there's nothing to it. The inhabitants who live near the khaadi have been using the surrounding open spaces, the rocky mounds and ditches for this only. No one feels anything about it. Only Savali is a darpoke, she dreads the open fields. Savali's mother says, Take her along. But Savali is, baap-re, so fussy. Not here, not there, she says and keeps walking till she finds a secluded corner. Aaliyo Savali, why walk so far? There are all kinds of insects – they might crawl up your leg! Savali would stop. She would squat behind a thicket, but if she heard the faintest sound of footsteps, she would get up at once. The vast open sky hanging over her head and the holes in the ground that looked like caves scared her.

She would panic. And every time it happened, she would remember her childhood when she was in the village. Savali's father would make her and her little brother Budhiya sleep on a cot outside their hut. She would wake up with a start suddenly in the night and find her father missing and the door of the hut closed. Far away, jackals howled, dry leaves rustled as they floated down from the topmost branch of the tree, something slithered into the bushes nearby and frightened Savali. The darkness would swallow her, she felt and even in the wintry night, she would break into a sweat. One night she had been so terrified that she ran to the hut and banged loudly on the door. Her father came out and finding nothing the matter, gave her a slap. Not very hard though, because he was still half-asleep. But after that, Savali was scared to even wake her father or mother. So in the dark night she would lie on the cot, wide awake, all alone, and very nervous. Budhiya was so young; he slept soundly, unaware of anything.

The Door

Here, in the city, everything was different. The slum was teeming with people, night and day. Amid the bustling crowds, everyone went out in the open, with a tumbler of water – it was a common sight. Nani kaki once took Savali to the public toilet. There was a queue outside, but there was one very good thing – the door could be closed. It was only when she went inside did she realize that the door was a door in name only. The latch was broken. Repeatedly, she had told Nani kaki and Panni to see that no one opened the door, but both of them were so busy gossiping that they forgot she was inside and a huge big man with a moustache pushed open the door. Savali just froze inside, overcome with shame and fear. When she stood up her legs were shaking. The rogue was standing outside, laughing. Savali thought he even winked at her. Whenever Savali saw him after that, she would turn away, embarrassed. Once, on Aatham night, a film was shown in Dayajinagar. Half of it Savali missed because she fell asleep but she remembered clearly the pink tiled bathroom and the heroine like a fairy covered with soap bubbles. Savanti said that bathrooms in the bungalows were like this only. That's why she must be working in a bungalow, thought Savali. Here, in the slum, they had four bamboos covered with a tattered sacking-cloth. You couldn't take off your clothes and pour water over your body. There was a constant fear that someone would peep in if they were not already watching. Behind was the factory road, cycles, scooters would go up and down, idle youth loitered around, whistling, like loafers. So even while you were inside, it was as if you were naked and bathing in front of all those people.

Savanti and Mumtaz had started menstruating five to six months ago and they said that during such days, it was such a big problem to go outside.

One had to control nature's calls, they said. Both of them worked in the bungalow so they often used the toilets there. Panni told Savali that it would happen to her also. Savali was shocked. That meant filth every month. And after that, who knows how much more mother will scold ... Already she said, "The fair lady wants soap everyday. Right now she is not bringing a single paisa into the house, yet she makes such a fuss. And the way she uses the soap, within a week, it becomes a thin, thin strip."

One day a big fair was held in the open ground near the khaadi. The slum dwellers thronged the place in large numbers. Since a couple of days, Panni and Savanti were persuading Savali to go with them but her mother was reluctant to let her go. She thought that Savali might spend the hard earned five rupees so it was better not to go ... Savanti had her own money so she had to ask no one. Eventually, Savali's mother agreed somehow, so Savali combed her hair tightly, applied layers of powder and holding Savanti's hand tight they mingled with the crowd. Mother had told her at least ten times that they should not let go of each other's hands, or else they would get lost in the crowd. And searching for each other would take the whole night. Don't wait till it becomes dark, don't stay around the same place for a long time, she had warned. The bangles and bindis stall had long queues and everyone was clamouring for them. All of a sudden there was a

The Door

stampede and with all the shrieking and confusion, no one knew what had happened. Savali got separated from Savanti. She screamed, shouted out her name, but in the noise she was not heard. As she stood there, alone, almost ready to cry, a kind-looking woman grabbed her hand. She took her out of the ground carefully, and made her sit down. She asked her who she was and where she lived.

"Dayajinagar? Come, I will take you there. Don't be afraid," she told Savali. Wiping her eyes on her sleeves, Savali started walking with the woman. "Let us take a rickshaw," the woman said and as they got in, she said, "First we'll just tell them at my place, then I'll take you to your house. You are not in a hurry, are you?"

She shook her head. The rickshaw went through some narrow galis and brightly lit, colourful shops and strange looking houses. Several doors were shut but many were open. Everything was strange, but she was not afraid. Must be because the woman was very kind.

The rickshaw stopped at a corner in front of a big building with a big porch, and intimidating doors. There was a courtyard in the centre and rooms all round it. A few windows opened and some faces peeped out from them. Wondering how many people must be living in this very big place, Savali stood there.

Sounds of singing and suppressed laughter were coming from somewhere, but nothing was visible. The doors of the rooms were shut tight and those that were open, had full length curtains with red and pink flowers, but nothing could be seen inside.

"I will just come, then we will go to leave you at your house." With that, the woman disappeared.

Savanti must be searching for her. Everyone must have already reached home by now and mother must be yelling ... See, I told you not to take her, now where will we find her in the huge crowds, such a frail child, must have been trampled upon by now ...

All of a sudden, Savali got a cramp in her stomach. She was a little hungry and thirsty and now, this convulsion in the stomach. Of course, she would get a cramp now, today it was the third day she had avoided going ... She would ask to be shown to the toilet once the woman came out. This big house must have everything, naturally ... Once it was finished, it would not bother her tomorrow.

The churning in her stomach became worse. She was confused and afraid, too. The kind woman would come out and she would ask her immediately where the toilet was. No one would mind such a request, surely. So she asked the woman.

"Yes, yes. Arre Munni, just show her ..."

On one side of the courtyard were two huge bathrooms, one with nice soft pink and the other with blue tiles. She immediately remembered the bathroom she had seen in the film. Absolutely clean, doors that could be closed properly, and proper concrete walls. And all these people would be using them everyday!

She kept looking at the door and the latch with absolute wonder in her eyes. When the door closes, then everything remains outside. We don't even get scared inside, no one can open it, on one can peep inside, no problems at all ...

The Door

"Go inside ..." the girl said to Savali.

Overcome with sheer joy, Savali was almost lifted off the ground. As if in a dream, she stepped inside. And the door closed behind her, really tightly.

Big Apple, BLACK APPLE

MRIDULA GARG

translated from Hindi by Shalini Sharma

I am an Indian. So are all my relatives, friends and acquaintances. One day I announced, "I am going to New York." Immediately, there was a shower of congratulations and a fair sprinkling of advice.

"The Big Apple ... how lucky you are! Wow!"

"No, no, New York."

"It's the same thing. Everybody's dream. The symbol of success. The Big Apple!"

Really, what a name! An entire city, red and healthy. Fair faces, bulging red cheeks.

"But beware of the blacks."

"Don't take the subway. There is a lot of violence caused by the blacks."

"Don't go towards Queens. It is full of blacks."

"Take care of your luggage. Those black rascals are all thieves."

That was the limit. Abusing me right to my face. I know I am dark. I have been hearing it since I was a child. I have grown tired of listening to it. Thank god for Peter Brooke's *Mahabharata*. That brought the blacks back into fashion. That is, talking about them has become fashionable, as exotic, ethnic, among other things. Till then all I ever rated was, "poor thing," that's it. The most they could ever say was, She has good features. If only she were fair. As if they themselves are fair.

Wheatish, almond, dusky complexioned – we have all possible shades of brown among us. But I am beyond even these accepted shades. I am just plain black. Black as a brinjal.

"What do you mean by blacks?" I could no longer control my anger.

"Negro. African. What else? But don't call them Negroes. They like being called blacks. The idiots say black is beautiful."

"Crazy. One has heard of black moles looking good on fair faces. But imagine being completely black. What a perception of beauty."

"Ha-ha, hee-hee, hoo-hoo," there was much laughter all around.

Black is beautiful. Black, beautiful? Is the apple black too? Black and beautiful. The wicked stepmother had fed Snow White a poisoned apple.

Was that the black apple? Maybe. Mr Dior of France has created a perfume called Poison. A black bottle in the shape of a half-cut apple.

It became so popular there. Here as well. Out of necessity.

Whatever the trend there, it has to be followed here. Black is Beautiful, isn't it? Then why not here, shall I ask them?

But they spoke before I could.

"It's a very expensive city. Where will you stay?"

"Take my nephew's address. He lives in the posh suburb, Chippequa. He earns a lot. Stay there. You can go to the Big Apple in the morning, and return in the evening." Shall I ask if the nephew is white or black? What a thing to ask! An Indian's nephew will be an

BIG APPLE, BLACK APPLE

Indian, right? Not really. Forget it. Whatever he is, my accommodation has been arranged. That's enough. Spoke to the nephew. I was told, "Enquire at JFK airport at New York and take a train to Chippequa station. Call me from there. I'll come and pick you up. Telephones here never go out-of-order."

Good.

I reached JFK airport. The Big Apple. Everything was big. Big airport. Big lounge. Big suitcase. Big men. Big women. Big Enquiry board. Very big. Visible from far.

Dragging the big suitcase behind me, I crossed the big lounge, reached the Enquiry counter and stood in front of a red cheeked, healthy, white woman.

"When does the train leave for Chippequa? And from where?"

"I don't know."

"You must have a timetable? Tourist information? Where can I get a train for Chippequa and when?"

"Honestly, I don't know."

"Where can I ask?"

"I honestly don't know."

"Please, how can I go to Chippequa?"

"Taxi."

"Besides taxi? Trains also go ... I was told to ask you."

"I told you, honestly, I don't know."

"So tell me dishonestly then."

"Move on. There's a queue behind you, can't you see?"

Looked back, saw the queue. People in the queue. Asked them too. Red men, like ripe apples. Pink women like delicious apples. Every time I got the same answer,

"Honestly, I don't know."

Oh god, isn't anyone dishonest here?

I was almost in tears. Called up Chippequa. I was advised, "Take a taxi and come. It will cost you about $40. What else can you do. Ask a policeman and get the fare fixed."

I had no choice. At least my hotel expenses had been saved. I walked towards the taxi stand. Saw taxis. Four. All the drivers were white, red. I was reassured. I reached one of the taxis. Said "Chippequa station."

"Metre or without metre?"

I remembered suddenly. I had been told to ask a policeman and then fix the fare. I saw one coming. But ... Black!

"Stay away from the blacks."

Oh god! Now? Should I forget it? But he was advancing towards me like a yamaduta, a messenger of Death.

"Any problem?" he asked. Such a tall, strong, black man. I was scared. My breath stuck in my throat. I managed to squeak, "The fare to Chippequa?"

"Start the metre," he said to the driver and to me, "It will come to about $30, okay?"

"Okay."

He walked away. What a sweet voice. I felt like stopping him. Asking him about the train. Maybe he is dishonest. But ... beware of blacks.

The driver was already in the car. He opened the boot of the car immediately. He must have pressed a button. Somehow, using all the strength that my slight frame could muster, I put the big suitcase in it. As soon as I flopped panting into the taxi, it moved off and immediately got stuck in a traffic jam.

Really, what speed! It may have stopped with a jerk, but it had started off like an arrow. What fun. Outside it was chilling cold, but inside the taxi it was warm enough to make you sweat. The temperature was more than comfortable. My eyes closed. They opened only when I heard the driver's voice.

"Where do you have to go?"

"Chippequa station."

"Where's that?"

"I don't know. Must be in Chippequa. That is, before it. Wait, I'll have a look at the map." As I opened the map I happened to glance at the metre. $40. Oh god! That means Chippequa has been left behind.

"We have passed Chippequa. He had said $30."

"Nonsense. Thirty! What does he know?"

"He was a policeman."

"So? Black swine. Get off here." The taxi stopped.

"How can I get down here? Let's go in to the town and ask. Look in the map. I have to go to Chippequa."

"It will cost you not less than 60 to 70 on the metre, understand?"

"Whatever. At least we'll get some information. Move on. A sign post might give us a clue about where we are. Then I'll look at the map."

The taxi was moving before I had finished my sentence. As if black thieves were after it. I couldn't read anything when I saw the board.

"Chippequa? Chippequa?" I shrieked.

"Street? Building number?"

"Nothing, let's just go to the station."

"Back to the station? Are you mad?"

"Not back. Chippequa station. Wherever it is – ahead or behind us."

Oh god, brave Hanuman, Sita-Ram, Radha-Krishan, Bholeshankar, Allah, Jesus, help me. Tell him where Chippequa station is.

The speeding taxi turned right. I looked around. There wasn't even the "C" of Chippequa in sight. The taxi stopped before I could say anything. The driver got down, "This way."

"Where?" It was deserted. There was a cemetery nearby. A building yard. On one side wood was being cut at lightning speed. Two fat, red-faced whites were handling the mechanical saw.

"This isn't the station."

"Why, isn't that the railway track?"

Yes, there was an abandoned rail line nearby.

"The presence of a rail line doesn't mean a station exists there."

It seemed almost like a profound spiritual statement to my trembling self. But not to him.

"Get down."

"No."

"Then go to hell."

He went into the yard. The three of them were drinking coffee and they kept looking towards me and laughing.

I heard, "The black bitch."

Where? Who? There was no one there. Only me. So was it me? Could they mean me? Oh merciful god ... the policeman ... Had he noted down the taxi number? Yes, he had.

"Remember, the police has your number. Take me

to the station." I roared, if a goat's voice can be termed a roar. He laughed, they all laughed a lot and then suddenly they stopped.

"What's happening?"

How did that black policeman come here? No, this is a different man. All blacks look alike, don't they?

"Nothing," both the red-faced men returned to their work immediately.

"Yes, son?" the black policeman asked the taxi driver, but the "son" was almost like a slap.

"Listen. Listen. Please, listen." I opened the door and shouted.

"Me? Sure." A whistle sounded and he was standing next to me.

He was like a monster. He laughed. His eyes laughed first, and then his lips. Lighting is always followed by thunder, isn't it?

"Yes, miss?"

Before I could decide whether to be scared of him or not, the other fear made me speak. "Please, help me. I have to go to Chippequa station. I don't know where he is taking me, please."

What was this? Asking a Black for help …

He stopped laughing.

He looked scary.

Sita-Ram! Sita-Ram!

The yamaduta opened the door of the car and sat next to me.

I shrank into a corner.

He blew the whistle.

Please, no! Oh god, Allah, Jesus, sweet Jesus, sweet Jesus!

The driver came running.

"Chippequa station. Straightaway. No fooling about," he said and got out, laughing.

My blood froze in my veins.

The driver was sweating. He turned the car around in the direction we had come from.

"Bastard! Pig!" he continued abusing, but he didn't slow down the car.

We reached Chippequa station. The name was written in such big letters – C-h-i-p-p-e-q-u-a. Aha! One could have reached it in half the time. But the metre read $70! This was murder. I had with me a total of $500 and here I was spending $70 on the first day itself. What lay ahead? I had a gold chain round my neck. I could sell it if I had to. Now they keep credit cards. But we have always worn gold. We'll see.

The taxi stopped. I got down, went to the back of the car. I was gathering my strength while the boot of the car was being opened. The boot remained shut.

"Open the boot," I cried out.

The driver got down. Arre, he was a young boy of twenty. My son's age. I was needlessly scared of him. Now, everything seemed normal except for the metre.

"Open the boot."

"Give me the money first."

"I'll give it to you when the bags are out."

"No, first the money."

"Why?"

"People run off without paying the fare."

"People run off on foot with the luggage and you can't follow them in a car?" I burst out laughing. The kid was mad.

"It happens with me."

"But how can a person on foot run faster than a car?"

"I don't know."

"Honestly."

"Yes!"

Who was I bantering with. Hearing voices, I gained courage and in a louder voice said, "I won't pay you until I get my luggage."

Nobody even slowed down their stride.

Taking my life in my hands, I stood in front of the car, holding on to the mudguard.

"Open the boot and take out my luggage, then take your money," I waved seven notes of $10 each in the air. "I have only this much cash." Nobody stopped even when I was screaming.

Big Apple – strong red-faced people passed by, unconcerned.

"Everybody cheats me," the boy was saying. But I was actually experiencing it.

I softened my voice, "Why do you think this way, son? Don't your parents love you?"

"What is it to you?"

"I am not cheating you. The black cop was wrong. This distance could never have come to only $30."

I waved the notes again. Shame. Accusing a stranger wrongly. But what could I do? Save my cash or my conscience?

The boot sprang open. I ran to the back. I had barely taken the big suitcase out when he snatched the money and started the car. I fell back with the suitcase. So what. I stood up, dusting myself. At least both my possessions and I were safe. What more could I ask for?

I called the nephew and he came and took me home. He listened to my story and said, "These black rascals are all cheats."

"You've understood it wrong. The driver was white. The policeman and the foreman were blacks."

"Maybe. The exception proves the rule."

Oh God! These clever sayings!

But who was going to say anything? I had managed to get a roof over my head with some difficulty. I didn't want to lose it because of what I said. I was ravenous too. I stuffed toast in my mouth and kept quiet.

Slept soundly.

The next day I wandered about the neighbourhood. Impressive place. Big houses. Wide grounds. Long cars. Monstrous coffee in big paper glasses. Everything was high, big, open, broad.

And white. The nephew said, "This is a good, posh colony. The best part is that no blacks live here. So no thefts or burglaries."

I heard it once. Twice. Again and again. I heard it while drinking coffee, while strolling in the mall, while shopping in the supermarket, while entering the house, while going out of the house. Finally, my irritation crossed the threshold of my patience. I said, "You mean, you are the only black here?"

"I am an Asian."

"Hanh, but even if you are considered fair in India, here all Indians must be considered equally black."

His face turned red, that is purple. Then pale, which means it turned dark. He couldn't say a word. Swallowing hard, he ate a whole big chocolate at one go.

Chocolate is black. And black is beautiful, my mind said. And you are mad. There was no need to open my mouth and lose a host. Now, what? The Big Apple. What else?

I spent the night there, somehow. The next morning found me at Chippequa station with my suitcase. To catch the train to New York. My work would take the entire day. I would have to find a room for the night.

The flight for Chicago was only the next morning ... I had a brother-in-law there. Absolutely black, Hindustani. He would not be able to throw me out of the house if I called him black. After all I am a relative.

The train arrived. The door of the coach was quite wide. I was the one who was clumsy, uneasy ...

I saw two empty seats. I walked towards them, breathing hard.

Letting go of the suitcase, I was about to flop down on the seat. But I couldn't.

The table which had been locked behind the seat fell open and hit me on my stomach. I remained standing like a deflated balloon.

"We are playing cards here," a fat, red-faced man said. He had dropped the table. The table was in the middle of the four seats. On two of the seats were big apple-like white men. Two were empty. The people in the compartment were enjoying the scene. They were all respectable people wearing formal suits and overcoats and holding briefcases. They must all be taking this train to the Big Apple every morning and returning together after work. They must be playing cards every day. But the same thing could have been said more politely ... I observed that all the educated there were whites. There were no blacks except me. The nephew had said, Chippequa didn't have any blacks. I wished the compartment had a few. I picked up my suitcase. Before going to the other seat, all I said was, "Are all Americans as uncivilized, or is it just you?"

Coward! Black coward! Sitting on the seat, I rebuked myself. If Gandhiji had been here he would have refused to give up the seat. He would have persisted despite being pushed about and beaten, until he was thrown out bodily by the people. He would not have worried about the suitcase. But I? Of the same nationality, yet ... The fact that I opened my mouth was absolutely fine. But why did I have to move? If I had stayed put, what could they have done? Killed me? So what? A person can be killed only once. But then that is the problem. That is what dying is. I felt like crying. But I didn't. Humiliation, self-condemnation, anger, shame, I conquered each one of them. Nobody can surpass me in getting into arguments with myself. There was no disrespect here. Think about the dalits who were not even allowed to enter a compartment. They didn't have money to buy tickets. And if they did, they huddled in a corner ... They hesitated to come near respectable people. Every moment of their lives were spent like this. They get kicks in their stomachs, not a mere table.

My humiliation was nothing compared to theirs. Honestly, it was nothing. But dishonestly?

The person I had to meet in New York lived in Manhattan, 10th street.

Five thirty in the evening was the time she had given me. I decided to stay somewhere within walking distance so that I could save on taxi fare.

"Don't get on the subway. The blacks are responsible for a lot of violence," I remembered the warning.

I took the cheapest room at the Best Western Hotel on 32nd Street. It was a very strange hotel. They made me first deposit some money, apparently for phone calls. There was quite a long queue.

I don't have to make any calls, I told them.

"Take back your money when you leave."

"In a queue?"

"Obviously."

What could I say? Developed countries had these kinds of rules.

I heard on television – there is an eighty per cent chance of a storm in the evening.

Chance! Don't I know it? When our weather department predicts the weather, we get absolutely the opposite. Bright sun instead of heavy rainfall. Heavy rainfall instead of a clear sky.

Dumping my suitcase in the room, I went out for a walk. It was the killing December cold. But sunny. No snow, no rain. I enjoyed the stroll. Sitting in a cafe on one side of the street, I ate a slice of pizza – that day's special cheap offer – drank tasteless coffee, looked inside shops and admired the goods in the windows. Looked from the top of the Empire State Building at the hazy scene below as if it was Chandni Chowk along the sea.

It started drizzling at three pm. I walked hurriedly towards the hotel. The drizzle stopped. A cold wind started blowing. I put on a coat over my sari and stepped into the lounge. I would stroll down to 10th Street once it turned four. It began to rain then. It will stop. If it doesn't,

I will take a taxi, I thought. I had an umbrella. The rain did not stop. It only became heavier. A sharp wind accompanied it. The door of the hotel was crowded with people waiting for taxis. Everyone was in a hurry. Every third person was desperate to reach the airport. I joined the crowd. After an hour's impatient wait, I got a cab. I settled into the seat and relaxed in the warmth of the cab. The scene outside was interesting. The wind was whipping and driving the rain.

The taxi was moving so slowly that it seemed to be stationary. But we were covering the distance somehow. Except for the blinding rain, nothing else was visible outside. And even if it was, I would not have recognized anything. It was absolutely alien to me. But I wasn't scared. After all, I only had to go from one street in Manhattan to another. Building number 42, 10th street, I told the driver and settled back without any fears or doubts.

The taxi turned into a lane and stopped. "If you get out in this rain, you will fall ill." It was nice to hear the black driver say it. Somehow holding on to my umbrella I was about to get out of the car when I saw the shining number on the building – 38, not 42.

"Not this one, it's further down," I said sitting down again.

"I am not going further."

"Why not?"

"Just like that. I am not going."

"But why? You'll take the fare according to the reading on the metre. What do you have to lose? It is only two buildings away."

"Either get down here, or we'll go back."

"In this rain?"

"Why did you come in the rain?"

"I had work. I had to come. Let's move, please."

"No."

"But why?"

"I'll get passengers more easily here."

"I'll fall ill if I step out in this rain. You said so yourself."

"That you definitely will. Should we return?"

"No."

"Then get off."

There was no time for arguments. I wanted to reach at five thirty. I didn't want to listen to things like, "Indians are never on time."

I got out and ran to take shelter under the portico. After a moment, I dashed out to the next portico. And in this way, getting wet from time to time, from number 38, I managed to reach number 42.

The rain continued to lash to the tune of the thunder. My hostess was surprised. How could anybody reach on time in this kind of weather. That too, at five thirty in the evening.

"Why, is this the most crowded hour of the day?" I asked her.

"Yes."

"At five thirty in the evening?"

"Yes."

Then why had she given me that time of the day? I had told her this was my first visit to New York. I knew nothing about this city.

I sneezed instead of asking her. Because of the high temperature in the room, my wet synthetic sari was giving out steam. Hell must look like this. She glared at me, and asked, "Coffee?"

I sneezed in reply. She poured the coffee from the decanter. I told her the story behind my drenched state and sneezes. She increased the temperature in the room.

"Be grateful he did not drop you at the turning into the street. Anything can happen here," she said.

"Specially at five thirty in the evening?"

"Absolutely." Her calm demeanour was worth appreciating.

I thought of asking her why she had, despite everything, fixed that particular time for me. But it seemed foolish to cool the already lukewarm coffee.

We started talking business.

My story was to be included in the anthology of Indian women's stories. The contract had to be signed. We exchanged views about the other stories and essays. She kept two of my essays with her. I gave her my brother-in-law's Chicago address for correspondence. Then I took leave. She shook my hands warmly, praised my sari and looked pointedly at the door. I asked, "Can't I call for a taxi from here?" She said, "The janitor in the hall downstairs will do it. There won't be any problem. Take care."

I thanked her.

There was a sickly looking black child in the hall. It felt good to see him. At least somebody was small in this big country. But as soon as I asked him to get me a taxi, he snarled, "Where will I get it? I will have to go out and yell for it just like you will. If you wanted to ask for a limo, you should have called from upstairs."

"Should I go upstairs?"

"If you want to pay four times the amount, then go."

"Will I get a taxi outside?" I bit my tongue as soon as the words left my mouth. Now he will say, honestly he doesn't know. He laughed. Could he read my mind?

"No problem. Take care."

I peeped outside. The rain seemed to have lessened its fury. I opened my umbrella and stepped over the threshold. My umbrella turned inside out with the first lash of the icy wind. My bones were freezing. I broke into a run to infuse some warmth into myself. On seeing a taxi, I ran so fast that had it been a stadium, I would have got the fastest woman award. "Taxi!" I called out.

The taxi driver said a cryptic "Off duty" and moved away. I moved on too, with the rain. So why would the wind lag behind?

I kept seeing taxis. I kept running up to them. The slogan of "Off duty" remained as popular. The battle between the rain and the wind continued. Running, stopping, walking, in every way, I kept getting wet, shivering, sneezing. In the race, sometimes the rain would take the lead, sometimes the wind. I lost to both of them. Soaking wet, sari sticking to a sweating, warm body was making it difficult to walk. Running was an entirely different proposition.

When I finally found a policeman, I pleaded with him too. It was a matter of just one taxi. Even half would do. I was desperate. I would give away all my money for a taxi.

What could the policeman have done anyway? It was a free country. The driver would go if he felt like, he wouldn't if he didn't want to.

I wandered all over, and when I couldn't find even

the half taxi I was looking for, I went back to 10th street, building number 42. I rang the bell of my hostess. I decided to ask her to call for a limo, whether she resented it or not. Even if the fare came to four or six times the usual. As I had said earlier, My kingdom for a horse!

There was no answer. The boy told me she had left immediately after me.

"She could have dropped me at a taxi stand if she was going out."

He shrugged and said, "You can't sit here. I'm locking up and going home."

"Do you have a car?"

He laughed.

"I live right here behind the building."

I was on the road again.

I could hear dogs and cats in the rain. Probably my imagination, affected by the English proverb. But the rain was merciless. It had a whip-like quality, exactly. The hand holding the whip was the rain, and the whip was the wind. Or maybe the hand was the wind and the whip was the rain, I couldn't be too sure. Whatever it was, it was killing me.

The chilling slippery feel of the wet sari on my burning skin was beyond endurance. My head was spinning. I was afraid I would collapse right in the middle of the road if I walked any further.

Like god incarnate, the edifice of the University of New York appeared in front of me, and I offered myself to it.

I entered the big hall. There was a sofa against the wall. One entire sofa, empty. Somehow or the other I stumbled up to it and sank down.

Everything stilled for a moment.

As soon as the icy wind stopped, the central heating enveloped me in warmth. The steam rose from my wet body and surrounded me. It seemed as if I was in a sauna bath.

The vapour rose like a curtain, layers of warm fog. My eyes were going misty in the cloud. People were disappearing in the haze. Only I remained, plunging, drowning, floating in the soft ocean.

I made a call ... the taxi arrived. I got into it ... I reached the room took off my sari ... lay down on the bed ... went off to sleep.

Don't sleep. Get up, make your call ... let me sleep ... I have just lain down ... I am wearing my clothes ... I just came in ... went off to sleep ...

Get up, wake up, call up.

Yes ... phone taxi ... I'll just do it ... I called up ... the taxi came ... I left ... reached ... lay down ... slept.

"Wake up, wake up!"

"Let me sleep."

"Get up."

"Let it be morning at least."

"Get up!"

I opened my eyes. A huge black monster was shaking me by my shoulder.

I screamed aloud.

He moved back, scared. He was taken aback.

I sat up.

He came near.

"Thank god, you're alive."

"Is this hell?"

"Yes, on Earth."

"Are you the devil?"

"Yes. Black. Male. And you?"

"Female. Black."

I started laughing and kept on laughing.

"Shut up," he scolded.

I stopped. Tears trickled down my cheeks.

"Why are you sitting here?"

"I could not find a taxi."

"Where do you have to go?"

"Best Western, Manhattan, 32nd street."

"Get up."

I got up. I stumbled against him. When I tried to cling to his T-shirt, I slid down. He held me up before I could reach the ground.

"Are you drunk?"

"No. Thirsty."

He touched my forehead, neck and then my hand.

"Are you an Indian?" I asked.

"No, African. You have fever."

"I don't know."

"Do you have an aspirin with you?"

"No."

"Come with me." He helped me to a cafe nearby, "Do you have money?"

"Yes."

"Two aspirins and two coffees. Give me the money."

I gave the money. He dissolved the tablet in water and said, "Drink it."

"On an empty stomach?"

He laughed. "No, kid, with a muffin."

I gave the money for the muffin. He handed me one. I took a mouthful and then I swallowed the aspirin.

"Let's go."

"Why? We will have our coffee at the table here."

"It will cost more unnecessarily. We will drink it on our way to the subway."

I saw two big plastic glasses with covers on them. Holding me with one hand, he had a muffin and the other coffee in his other hand. He took off the cover with his teeth and started drinking it as he walked. I was moving on my own.

"The lid!" I burst out and couldn't stop laughing.

"What is it?"

"Glass ... lid." I continued laughing.

"Eat your muffin quickly." He too was laughing. He held his muffin between his teeth and asked me, "Do you want this too?"

"No."

He nibbled at his muffin. So big, like a cauliflower. "Big Apple!" I laughed.

"Drink your coffee," he forced me to take a sip of the coffee.

"Hold."

I held the glass.

"Keep walking."

How could I stop? He was pushing me.

The rain had stopped.

"What's the time?" I asked.

"Four."

"Four? Then why is it so dark?"

"It's four in the night."

"Night ... you mean, morning?"

He laughed. "Morning ... night ... it's night whenever it is dark."

My laughter disappeared. He continued pushing me ahead.

"Straight ahead is the subway station. Board the train and get down at the third stop. You'll find Best Western right there. Understand?"

"And you?"

"I'll come till the station."

"I won't go alone in the subway."

"Why?"

"Blacks are bad, they create trouble."

"Then scoot. I am black too." It was his turn to burst into laughter. As soon as he removed his hand, I pulled it back.

"I feel scared."

"Of me? Then run away."

"No, of the big red apples."

"What red apples?"

"There are only worms here. I am black. You are black. The muffin is black. Coffee is black. Bees are black, so are houseflies. All worms are black."

He started singing, and soon his feet were also tapping. Even I did. He was sweeping me towards the subway.

We reached the station. He took money from me and bought a ticket from the machine. Handing it to me he said, "Go, your train is about to come."

The train arrived. I entered the compartment. It was half empty.

Half the seats had tired people all over. Some were black, some brown, a few even white. But all of them were similarly exhausted. Shrivelled. Like the Indian ber fruit.

On reaching the hotel, I crashed out and got up only when the alarm went off at twelve noon. I vacated the room, gathered my luggage, handed over the key, took my telephone money back, and bought two aspirins with coffee and a muffin.

I drank my coffee standing. I ate the muffin, swallowed my aspirin, and boarding the subway, left for the airport. One more worm had crawled out of the Big Apple.

"Big Apple, Black Apple" was first published as "Bada Seb, Kala Seb" in Hindi in *Dharmyug* in October 1992.

Bio-notes

Ahmad Yusuf started writing when he was eighteen years old and has several collections to his credit.

Nadeem Ahmed has an MBA and is fluent in Urdu, Hindi and French.

Ahmed Nadeem Qasmi was born in 1916 and has written many stories and poems in Urdu and Punjabi. His writings have been collected in twelve volumes. His best-known collection of stories are *Neela Pathar* and *Aas Paas*.

Sufiya Pathan has an MA in English from SNDT University, Mumbai. She is an active participant of the KATHA-SNDT Translation Programme.

Bolwar Mahamad Kunhi is the first writer to depict the travails of Muslims, in Kannada literature. He has to his credit four short story collections, a novel and two documentaries. Among them are *Devarugalla Rajyadalli* which won the Karnataka Sahitya Akademi Award (1983), *Anka* a collection of short stories which won the Bharatiya Bhasha Sansthan Award (1986), and *Akashakke Neeli Parade* which won the Sahitya Akademi Award for the Best Creative Book (1992).

H Y Sharada Prasad was Information Advisor to the late prime minister, Rajiv Gandhi. He has translated Shivaram Karanth's novels from Kannada into English and also R K Narayan's *Swami and Friends* from English into Kannada.

Gita Krishnankutty is a writer of short stories as well as one of the leading translators of Malayalam fiction. She taught French at the Alliance Francais for many years.

Himanshi Shelat had her first collection of short stories, *Antaral*, published in 1987. It received the Gujarat Sahitya Parishad Award. She has written a number of short stories, two books for children, two novellas besides a monograph on surrealism and a few memoirs in the form of personal essays.

Darshana Dave has a Bachelor's degree in English Literature and is presently doing her second year of the Diploma in Journalism from the Xavier's Institute of Communication, Mumbai.

Mahasweta Devi is one of the foremost writers in Bangla and is a social activist committed to the welfare of tribal communities. She wrote her first novel, *Jhansir Rani*, in 1956. She has been honoured with several prestigious awards like the Sahitya Akademi Award (1979) for her work.

Mridula Nath Chakraborty teaches English and is currently working on her PhD at the University of Alberta, Canada. She is interested in 19th century world literature, traditional Indian recipes and Kishore Kumar memorabilia.

Mridula Garg was born in 1938 and has a Master's degree in Economics from the Delhi School of Economics. She has won the Maharaja Vir Singh Puraskar from the Madhya Pradesh Sahitya Parishad in 1975 and the Delhi Hindi Academy Sahityakar Samman in 1991. She has many novels to her name, besides a number of short stories. She has also translated a few Hindi novels and stories into English.

Swayam Prakash was born in 1947 in Indore, Madhya Pradesh. He has a Diploma in Mechanical Engineering. He has a number of short story collections to his name among which the best-known collections are *Charchit Kahaniya, Aadmi Jaat Ka Aadmi,* and *Ayenge Achche Din Bhi.* He was awarded the Rajasthan Sahitya Akademi Puraskar for the collection *Suraj Kab Niklega.* He has also written two novels, *Beech Me Vinay* and *Uttar Jeevan Katha.*

Madhavi Mahadevan, an experienced copy-writer, prefers writing, especially for children, and has had several short stories published in various children's magazines.

Kaveri Rastogi has an MA in English from Fergusson College, Pune. She has taught in various schools. She worked at Katha for a short while and is now teaching in a school in Delhi.

Vaikom Muhammad Basheer is one of Kerala's best-loved writers as well as one of the major influences on Malayalam literature. A versatile writer, he has written seventy five short stories, thirteen novels, two memoirs and a play. In recognition of his considerable contribution, he was conferred a fellowship by the Sahitya Akademi in 1970.

C P A Vasudevan is a retired Commissioner of Income Tax. He contributes stories, poems, articles and book reviews to leading newspapers and journals.

ABOUT KATHA

Katha is a registered nonprofit organization working in the area of creative communication for development. Katha's main objective is to enhance the pleasures of reading amongst children and adults.

Kalpavriksham, Katha's Centre for Sustainable Learning, is active in the field of education. It develops and publishes quality material in the literacy to literature spectrum, and works with an eye to excellence in education – from nonformal education of working children to formal education, from primary through higher education. Katha also works with teachers to help them make their teaching more creative. It publishes learning packages for first-generation schoolgoers and adult neo-literates. Specially designed for use in nonformal education, every quarter Katha brings out *Tamasha!*, a fun and activity magazine on development issues for children, in Hindi and English. The *Katha Vachak* series is an attempt to take fiction to neo-literates, especially women.

Katha-Khazana, part of Kalpavriksham, was started in Govindpuri, one of Delhi's largest slum clusters, in 1990. Kathashala and the Katha School of Entrepreneurship have over 1000 students – mostly working children. To enhance their futures, an income-generation programme for the women of this community – Shakti-Khazana – and the Khazana Women's Cooperative were also started in 1990.

The Katha National Institute of Translation strives to help forge linkages between writers, students and teachers. Launched in 1997 as Kanchi, KNIT has been conducting workshops in schools and colleges all over the country to enhance the pool of translators, editors and teachers of translated fiction. KNIT operates through five Academic Centres in various universities in the country – Bangalore University, IRIS, Jaipur, North East Hill University, Shillong, SNDT Women's University, Mumbai, in addition to its Delhi Centre.

Katha Vilasam, the Story Research and Resource Centre, seeks to foster and applaud quality fiction from the regional languages and take it to a wider readership through translations. The Katha Awards were instituted in 1990. Through projects like the Translation Contests, it attempts to build a bank of sensitive translators. KathaNet, an invaluable network of Friends of Katha, is the mainstay of all Katha Vilasam efforts. Katha Vilasam publications also include exciting books from Kathakaar, the Centre for Children's Literature which brings out the Yuvakatha and Balkatha series, for young adults and children respectively.

Be a Friend of Katha!

If you feel strongly about Indian literature, you belong with us! KathaNet, an invaluable network of our friends, is the mainstay of all our translation-related activities. We are happy to invite you to join this ever-widening circle of translation activists. Katha, with limited financial resources, is propped up by the unqualified enthusiasm and the indispensable support of nearly 5000 dedicated women and men.

We are constantly on the lookout for people who can spare the time to find stories for us, and to translate them. Katha has been able to access mainly the literature of the major Indian languages. Our efforts to locate resource people who could make the lesser-known literatures available to us have not yielded satisfactory results. We are specially eager to find Friends who could introduce us to Bhojpuri, Dogri, Kashmiri, Nepali and Sindhi fiction.

Do write to us with details about yourself, your language skills, the ways in which you can help us, and any material that you already have and feel might be publishable under a Katha programme. All this would be a labour of love, of course! But we do offer a discount of 20% on all our publications to Friends of Katha.

Write to us at –
Katha
A-3 Sarvodaya Enclave
Sri Aurobindo Marg
New Delhi 110 017
Fax: 651 4373
E-mail: katha@vsnl.com
Internet address: http//www.katha.org
Or call us at: 686 8193, 652 1752

Also from the House of Tamasha!
A fascinating tale of The Princesss with the Longest Hair

" ...One silent night, Parineeta quickly left her room. Through empty passages and down dark staircases she reached a door in the palace wall and..."

Where did Parineeta go??
Get your copy today for Rs 120.

OTHER BOOKS FROM THE HOUSE OF TAMASHA!

Crocodile And Other Stories
ISBN 81-85586-86-1

On A Sunny Shiny Night And Other Poems
ISBN 81-85586-87-X

Reach For The Moon!
ISBN 81-85586-88-8

The Elephant s Child And Other Stories
ISBN 81-85586-89-6

Tigers Forever And Other Poems
ISBN 81-85586-90-X

The World Around Us!
ISBN 81-85586-91-8

Price: Rs 25 each.
Special price: Rs 60 for a set of 3 books

Send your order to: Katha, A-3 Sarvodaya Enclave, Sri Aurobindo Marg, New Delhi 110 017.
Phone: 011-6868193, 6521752   Fax: 011-6514373   E-mail: katha@vsnl.com